Secret of
Pirates' Cave

Secret of Pirates' Cave

Dayle Courtney

STANDARD PUBLISHING
Cincinnati, Ohio

Thorne Twins Adventure Books

Jaws of Terror
The House That Ate People
The Great UFO Chase
Secret of Pirates' Cave

Library of Congress Cataloging-in-Publication Data

Courtney, Dayle.
    Secret of Pirates' Cave / Dayle Courtney.
        p. cm. — (Thorne Twins adventure books)
    Summary: The Thorne twins search for a buried treasure
stolen from their ancestors, but the ghost of a pirate emerges
from the shadows to protect "his" treasure.
    ISBN 0-87403-834-0
    [1. Buried treasure—Fiction. 2. Ghosts—Fiction. 3.
Pirates—Fiction. 4. Twins—Fiction.] I. Title. II. Series:
Courtney, Dayle. Thorne Twins adventure books.
PZ7.C83158Se 1991
[Fic]—dc20   91-11135
                                                 CIP
                                                  AC

Revised copyright © 1991, The STANDARD PUBLISHING
    Company, Cincinnati, Ohio.
A division of STANDEX INTERNATIONAL Corporation.
Printed in U.S.A.

Contents

1	Pirates!	7
2	Where Is the Treasure?	14
3	The Castle	21
4	The Search	29
5	The Secret Passage	37
6	A Cry in the Cavern	44
7	A New Plan	51
8	The Caves	58
9	Scarab's Directions	67
10	The Pirate's Grave	75
11	The Ghost	84
12	The Hidden Staircase	92
13	Star	99
14	In the Crypt	105
15	The Treasure	114
16	A Strange Message	121
17	The Meeting	129
18	Voice from the Past	136
19	A Difficult Decision	143
20	The Cave of the Monster	149
21	Greed Find Its Reward	156

1 • Pirates!

The four-masted schooner drifted through the fog, its limp sails shimmering like pale ghosts. Only the swish of the waves against its bow told that it moved at all.

Eric Thorne peered upward through the gray mist. He could feel a faint breeze now, against his face, and he wished that it would fill the sails and speed the ship forward again. When the boards creaked suddenly and began to groan, he could just make out the sail above them puffing outward. "Thank the Lord," he said to John Roberts, standing next to him at the ship's rail. "When the wind died this morning I feared we would be becalmed here in these strange seas."

Most of those who left Europe that year, 1850, were going to California hoping to find gold. But he and John, with their wives and young children, meant to build homes and settle in this New World. Now they were probably within sight of the coast.

"This fog hides everything," John grumbled. "'Tis hardly noon, yet it seems like night. We'll run aground and sink before we even see California."

Eric stroked his curly black beard thoughtfully.

"Captain Stuart has brought us all the way from England, through bad weather and good. I trust he will take us the short distance left just as safely."

"All the same, I have no stomach for fog. I'd rather be down in the cabin with the women and children, where at least I can see the four walls." John moved away, into the enveloping gray mist.

Eric stood alone, listening. It seemed he could hear faint voices across the water. A trick of the fog, probably. It could only be the sounds of the captain and crew in the bridge, or even the children in the cabins below.

The ship lurched, and there was a loud grinding noise. The deck seemed to drop from under his feet. He grabbed instinctively for the rail, but his fingers were jerked away as he fell. Now he was tumbling across the damp boards of the deck, helpless to stop himself.

His shoulder hit something solid. He was conscious of many voices shouting before he was sent sliding away again as the ship gave another heave. He vainly searched for something to stop himself, wondering if he would be dropped off this teeter-totter into the dark waters.

Then his body hit something yielding and he heard John shout with pain. Two hands fastened to the sleeve of his coat. "What's happening?" John dug his fingers into Eric's arm.

Eric had no breath to tell him he didn't know, but the weight of their two bodies together slowed their sliding. And it seemed the ship's rocking was growing less. Still it was some time before the deck was stable enough for the two men to sit up.

Eric looked around, feeling sore and dazed. He could see debris littering the deck near him. Above him, the captain shouted frantic orders to his crew. Eric managed to get up, rubbing his bruised shoulder.

John, too, was struggling to his feet. "We hit the rocks," he said mournfully. "Just as I feared."

Eric held his aching shoulder and moved his arm. Nothing seemed to be broken, at any rate. Just a throbbing in his hip and pain in his head. "Are you all right?" he asked his friend.

"Sound enough." John shook his head, the damp brown hair flopping around his ears. "I wonder how long we have before we sink?"

For a moment Eric wondered if he could be right. The women and children would have to be rescued from the cabin and set in a longboat. He started for the companionway, but already the door was opening and his wife was emerging, her face pale.

"Eric! Thank God you're all right! What was that awful crash?"

"We hit something, I'm sure. But you, Emily, and the children?"

"All of us were frightened but unharmed." She looked at John. "As are Catherine and your children. I told them to stay below until I could find out if there was danger."

"I fear we are sinking," John told her gloomily.

But Eric shook his head. "I doubt it. We seem to be riding as high and as level as before." He looked around and saw two deck hands nearby, clearing the litter and fastening bundles securely under ropes once more. "Seaman!" he called to the closest. "What happened?"

"The ship grazed something, Sir," the man called back. "When the fog lifts we can tell what it was."

"Is the ship damaged?"

"Some of the men are below now, Sir, to see if we're taking on water."

John frowned. "I think we should find the captain and ask him, just to be sure."

Eric took Emily's hand and they all headed for the bridge. He noticed that the fog had lifted enough now so they could see sparkles of sunlight on the waves. And then, as they paused by the rail, he saw something else.

9

It loomed dark and ghostlike, shrouded in mist, but Eric could see the painted figure of a woman leaning forward under the bow and the black sail that rose above it. Another ship closed swiftly behind them, the sun shimmering on the cannon that nosed out of its sides. He gasped and pointed. Beside him, Emily gave a small, frightened cry.

"What ships raise black sails?" Eric felt his heart begin a slow, heavy pounding.

"What standard does it fly?" John leaned forward, peering at the huge hull that surged toward them.

And in a moment, they could all see it. On the top of the forward masts, it fluttered its black insignia clearly. A skull and crossbones!

The captain and crew of their schooner had seen it, too. Men pounded to the bridge, shouting their fear.

"Go below, Emily," Eric told her, trying to stay calm. "It will be safer for you there."

"I don't want to leave you."

"Please, Emily—" But even as Eric spoke, a barrage of cannon fire overwhelmed his words. The schooner quivered, the mizzenmast splintered and crashed. As the ship rocked helplessly, Eric headed for the bridge, with John and Emily following.

Captain Stuart shoved a pistol into each man's hand, looking grim. "Get inside the wheelhouse, Ma'am," he told Emily. "We'll have to fight for our lives."

In a moment the air was blue with gunsmoke, as the crew fired at the pirates who were throwing grappling hooks down from the deck of their ship. The gunfire was deafening, but Eric could still hear the triumphant shrieks of the pirates as they swarmed down the ropes to land on the schooner's deck. He took shelter behind a bulkhead to reload his pistol. The pirates were vicious fighters. They were using knives, pistols, fists, and even swords. In too short a time there were wounded and dead all over the deck, and others of the schooner's crew were bound hand

and foot and set against the rail, while several of the victors rushed to the bridge.

Eric knelt behind the bulkhead, firing, with John a short distance away. The captain and his officers bravely tried to keep the pirates off the bridge, but it was no use. The invaders killed two men close to Eric, and as he watched, a burly pirate picked up the bosun's mate and hurled him to the deck below. As Eric stared in horror he was grabbed from behind, the pistol shaken from his hand, and he was dragged painfully by his feet across the deck. As soon as the hands released him, he sat up to see John, Captain Stuart, and several officers lined up against the wheelhouse, helpless prisoners.

"Get up!" said his captor, a round man whose wispy blond hair stuck out from under a woolen cap.

Dazed and frightened, Eric got to his feet and stood next to John, who had a cut across his cheek that was dripping blood. John dabbed at his wound with his palm, glaring silently around him.

The pirate captain came forward and stood before them. He was tall and well-muscled, with long, matted red hair. His face and arms were scarred and one of his front teeth was missing, but his eyes were clear, green, and amused. He wore dark green velvet breeches and a ruffled shirt with the sleeves cut off, and his boots were fine leather, though worn. Probably, Eric thought, clothes taken from some poor soul on another ship he'd robbed.

He took off his plumed green hat, scratched the top of his head, and grinned at them. "I'd never have known you were near if your ship hadn't nudged mine in the fog."

So that was the crash they'd felt!

Captain Stuart spoke bravely. "It was only an unlucky accident."

"Unlucky for you." The pirate's voice was smooth. "This tub left a scratch the whole length of our starboard side. And after we'd painted her all trim and shipshape, too."

11

Captain Stuart frowned. "What do you want with us?"

Some of the pirates standing behind their leader laughed and jeered. "Set him to painting the *Scarlet Bird* all over again, Scarab!"

The pirate chief winked to his men, then waved his right hand for silence. Eric saw that he wore a huge ring on his forefinger, with a single emerald carved in the shape of a beetle.

"What I want," Scarab told the captain, "is everything you've got on this ship. Everything of value."

"We have nothing valuable," Captain Stuart said quickly. "A few goods in the hold for the settlers in California. Some fabrics, a bit of furniture. None of it worth your time."

Scarab scowled at him. "I'll be the judge of that." He turned to his men. "Pete, Jonah, stay here. The rest of you search this tub from stem to stern."

Eric shivered with terror. Emily was still huddled in the wheelhouse, and below were his children and John's family. He glanced at John and saw the same fear on his face. What could they do? He took a step toward the pirate. "There are women and children on board," he said fiercely. "Are you so corrupt that you would cause them fear and pain? Leave this ship at once!"

Scarab smiled as he looked him up and down. "Passengers, are you? With your families?"

"Yes. I'm Eric Thorne. This is John Roberts. We are only peaceful settlers—"

The pirate reached out swiftly and yanked the gold chain from his neck. Eric winced from the sudden pain and rubbed his neck as Scarab held the chain up, looking at the gold and ruby cross that hung on it. "A pretty bauble for a poor settler," he said mockingly.

Eric made a grab to retrieve it, but Scarab's two men were beside him in a minute and pinioned his arms behind his back.

"Now, Eric Thorne, and John Roberts—give me those rings you wear. Quickly. Both of you."

And so Eric and John were forced to give him their rings, and John handed over the watch he wore on a golden fob. Eric was sick at the thought of this thief taking the cross that had been given to his great-grandfather by King George II, but he knew there was no use to object. These pirates would take all they had brought with them. He thought of the chest lying in the hold that held his family treasures . . . the beaten silver trays, the jeweled sword, and all the clocks and pictures that had been prized and kept safe for so many years. They were valuable, yes, but to Eric and Emily they were priceless because of the family memories they stood for. And then, of course, there was Emily's beads and necklaces, bracelets and rings—her heirlooms, which would have been passed on to their own children. And their small store of gold coins that they'd saved so carefully to help them get started in this New World. These would all be taken from them now. Still as long as they could all come through unharmed. . . .

His heart was pounding. He prayed silently, pleading with God that they would be left alive. The treasure he already counted as a loss. If he had depended on his wealth to see them through their journey to this new land, he had misplaced his faith. Now he was left with only God to help him, the only One who really ever could in the first place.

All the while, he studied this rough, lawless pirate who held them helpless in his power. What caused him to make his living this way, killing and robbing others of what was rightfully theirs? How could he live with himself?

"Now, Eric Thorne," Scarab said, coming toward him. "Where are the women and children hid?"

13

2 • Where Is the Treasure?

More than a hundred and forty years later, another Eric Thorne sat down with his family to their evening meal in their home in Ivy, Illinois.

"Pass the mashed potatoes, Alison," he asked his twin sister, who sat across from him. Then, as he heaped potatoes onto his plate, he looked toward his father. "Dad, something really weird happened today at school."

"Don't tell me you got an A in trigonometry!" Dr. Randall Thorne smiled.

"No. . . . I mean, finals aren't until next week, June the fifth. Anyway, there's this guy in my English class, Terry Roberts. He and his folks moved here a couple of months ago from California." He paused to take a mouthful of fried chicken.

"That doesn't sound weird to me," Aunt Rose said with a straight face. "Now, if he'd moved here from Mars, *that* would be weird."

They usually didn't have both Dad and Aunt Rose staying with them at the same time. Usually she stayed with the twins when their father was on one of his trips abroad working for the International Agricultural

14

Foundation. The twins' mother had died years before, when they were little.

"OK," Eric said. "You're all being very funny, but wait till you hear this. We had an assignment to write a composition about somebody in our family, and Terry wrote about one of his ancestors who came from England. What's so weird is that another family came over on the same ship. Their name was Thorne."

"Really?" Alison's brown eyes widened with surprise.

"Could they be related to us, Dad?" Eric asked. "Our family did come to America around then."

"Could be. . . ." He spoke to the dark-haired woman at the other end of the table. "Rose, do you remember the story?"

"Of course I remember!" Aunt Rose's face glowed with excitement.

"What story?" Eric asked, mystified.

"Did Terry say the ship was plundered by pirates?" asked Dad.

"That's right! How did you know?"

"Did he mention the name of the ship? Or the name of the pirate captain?"

"Scarab. That was the pirate's name. It means a kind of beetle, which I thought was pretty strange. He didn't say the name of the ship. His ancestor's name was John Roberts."

"Randall, they must be the same!" Aunt Rose exclaimed. "Wouldn't that be wonderful?"

He smiled. "Eric, you just might have made an important discovery. Did Terry say what year this happened?"

Eric frowned, trying to remember. "I think he said 1850."

"That's the right year!" said Aunt Rose.

"Why? What's so important?" Eric pushed his plate aside impatiently. "Tell us!"

15

"All right. If you're finished eating, we'll go into the study. I have to show you."

"I made angel food cake for dessert," Aunt Rose said. "We can bring it in with us."

They went to a small room at the front of the house, with a large cherrywood desk and many bookshelves. When they were all settled in their chairs with their cake and milk, Dad opened a drawer in the desk and pulled out a ring of keys. He unlocked a carved cabinet. "I'm sure this is where it is," he murmured. "I haven't seen it in years, but if I remember correctly . . ." He pulled out an oblong metal box, opened the lid, and grinned triumphantly. "Aha! I was right."

"What is it, Dad?" Alison tossed back her long, dark hair and watched him curiously.

"A letter. And something else." Her father placed the closed metal box on the desk and sat down. "First, the story. It was in 1850 when our ancestors, Eric and Emily Thorne and their three children, set sail on the schooner *Dartford* with all their belongings to make their home in California."

"Eric? Was I named after him?"

"You were named after my grandfather, who might have been named for him, I don't know," said Dad. "To continue, another family, by the name of Roberts, booked passage on the same ship. But close to the California coast, the *Dartford* was spotted by pirates. The pirate chief, known as Scarab, looted the ship, taking everything of value. Among the treasures he took was an ancient cross of gold studded with rubies that had been given to one of the Thorne forebears by a king of England. There was also, I understand, a family Bible and many family portraits, as well as silver and jewelry."

"Our ancestors were rich?" Alison asked him.

"I believe they had moderate wealth they worked hard for. And the pirates took it all, though they left both families unharmed, and the *Dartford* went on to land in California. The Thorne family lived in San Francisco until about 1880. After that, they moved here to Illinois, and they've been here ever since."

"Then the Roberts family must have stayed in California," Eric said. "Terry's family moved here from Monterey when his father got transferred. But what about the letter in the box? How does that fit in?"

"Did Terry's composition mention a letter?"

Eric shook his head. "All he wrote about was the pirates raiding the ship and taking everything. Let me guess—the letter tells where the treasure's hidden, right?"

"That's right."

"It does?" Alison whooped.

"But then why—" Eric began, but his twin finished the sentence.

"—haven't we found it by now? Where is it?"

"It's not all ours," Aunt Rose said quietly. "The Roberts family had their goods stolen, too."

Mr. Thorne rubbed the bridge of his nose thoughtfully. "After robbing the *Dartford*, apparently the pirate chief changed his evil ways. No one ever found him. He settled down to an ordinary life and never went to sea again, and he turned to God and repented of his sins. He also wrote two letters—one to our ancestor, Eric Thorne, and one to John Roberts. Our letter is right here."

He pulled a sheet of heavy, yellowed paper from the box. Eric craned his neck to look at it. It was crowded with faint, brownish writing.

"I can't pass it around," Dad said. "The paper is very old and brittle."

"When was it sent?" Eric asked.

"Well, I'm not sure of the exact date, but it must have been in the mid-1800's, while the Thornes were still living in San Francisco." Dad took a pair of glasses from the pocket of his tweed jacket, put them on, and began to read, faltering every now and then over a word that was hard to decipher.

Here is Scarab the pirate, which is the only one of my names I will tell you. Be it known to you that I write the same words to John Roberts, who sailed on the schooner Dartford with you.

I gave up my career of piracy after you prayed for my conversion even as I robbed you. Having found God, and having sincerely repented of my sins of murder and robbery and piracy on the high seas, and other crimes known only to myself and my Creator, I now would prove my true intention to make amends by giving back the gold and jewels I took from you by means of force.

Accompanying this letter is one half of a page of instructions I have drawn up by my own hand. I will send the other half to John Roberts, whose treasure is hidden with yours. Put the two halves together and you will know where to find it. By this means you will recover every piece of valuable property I took from you. It is up to you to separate them fairly.

I only regret that so many years have passed before I could think of a way to do this. Now my soul is, at least in some measure, at peace.

Mr. Thorne looked up from the letter. "He signs it, 'Forgive me,' and there is a drawing of a scarab beetle as his signature." He held the paper out so all could see it.

Excitement coursed through Eric. "Let's see those instructions, Dad! All we have to do now is get the Roberts's half and we'll have all our family treasure back again!"

Alison looked excited too, but doubtful. "Wait a minute Eric. If that's all there is to it, why didn't Dad's grandfather find it, or Gramps?"

"Did they?" Eric asked his father.

"No. That's the whole point. Your grandfather and his father both searched for the descendants of John Roberts, though they found many people named Roberts—even some families living on the California coast—but none of them could come up with the other half of the directions."

"But whatever Roberts has the other half must have been looking for the Thorne family, too."

"They probably found as many Thornes through the years as we found Robertses. But you've got to consider, Eric, that close to a century has passed. The letter and instructions that were sent to the original Roberts family might have been misplaced or lost entirely."

"I wonder," Aunt Rose said, "why Scarab knew where to send both letters, and yet the two families couldn't find each other?"

"My guess is that Scarab was determined to return the treasure, and he worked very hard to track both families down." Dad took off his reading glasses. "There would have been labels on the family goods, you know, showing the names and destination. And San Francisco in the 1800's would have been far less populated than it is now. But why the Roberts family and ours couldn't find each other is something I don't know."

"Can we see the directions now?" Eric asked.

Mr. Thorne took a document from the metal box, handling it carefully. It was preserved under glass in a leather frame. He handed it to Eric, and Alison moved so that she could see it, too. It was a half sheet with one torn edge. The words were written in the same brownish handwriting, and some of the letters were faded and missing at the torn border.

Lat. 37º
There is a road leadin
fort. Follow it southwe

boulder rises from the
of a lion's head. Turn t
of trees and you will fi
no great size but well a
Sunday. Go on or near
day. Find the stained
like a rose with a blue
the blue light will poin
the wall. Push against
will be revealed. Look
means a star. Under t
your entire fortunes w
When you do, my soul
torment.

"You can almost tell what the other half says," Eric pointed out. "There's a fort, and a boulder shaped like a lion's head."

"But what fort?" Alison said. "There must be a lot of old forts all across the country."

"But look, it gives the latitude."

"Which is not much good without the longitude, is it, Dad?" Alison looked up.

"Well, if you assume it's along the west coast of the United States, we can be pretty sure of the area. That would be a reasonable guess, in any case."

"But the rest of the directions don't make much sense," Eric said. "I mean, why 'Sunday,' and what's this 'blue light'?" He looked at his father. "Why don't we talk to Terry and his folks? Maybe they really do have the other half of this paper."

"We can certainly try."

"Let's phone them right now and invite them over for cake," Aunt Rose suggested. She looked at the untouched plates on the desk. "There's lots of it left."

3 • The Castle

Terry's father shook his head. "My father told me the story of the piracy, but he never mentioned a letter."

Mr. and Mrs. Roberts sat in the living room with a plate of Aunt Rose's angel food cake in his hands. Terry, a blue-eyed, brown-haired sixteen-year-old, perched on the arm of the couch, a look of curiosity on his tanned face.

"Let me read you ours," Mr. Thorne said. While he read the letter to them, Terry and his parents looked at the half page of directions on the coffee table in front of them. When Mr. Thorne was finished, they looked questioningly at each other.

"Scarab," Mr. Roberts said. "I remember that very well. It's an unusual name."

"Would Uncle Dan know about the letter?" Terry asked. "Or Aunt Barbara?"

"Not as far as I know. If it was ever received, it must have been lost a long time ago." Mr. Roberts turned to the others. "Barbara is my older sister. She's a widow and has been living in my parents' house with her son, James, ever since my father passed away. Dan is my brother and he lives close by, in Monterey, California."

21

"Maybe your parents had the letter and stored it some-place in their house," Eric suggested.

"I'm sure they would have told us about it," Mr. Roberts said. "Although that is a possibility."

"Wouldn't it be great if we could find our half of the directions and get the treasure back?" Terry said dreamily.

"If it's still wherever Scarab put it," Alison said. "It might not be, after all this time. Somebody else could have found it long ago, even without the directions."

"I think Scarab would have been smart enough to hide it better than that," Eric said. "I'm sure it's still there. There's lots of buried treasure around."

Mrs. Roberts spoke to her husband. "Surely someone would have mentioned it through the years. And wouldn't one of your family have tried to find the Thornes who had the other half?"

Mr. Roberts just shook his head.

"Well," Mr. Thorne said. "I must admit that I've let these documents lie in the box for years without doing a thing about them. I might have forgotten them entirely if Eric hadn't mentioned Terry's composition this evening."

"I think everyone took it for granted that all efforts had been made," Aunt Rose said. "We all thought of it as an-cient history, until now."

"And now it's possible, isn't it?" Eric didn't want to give up. The prospect of finding the treasure was too exciting. "We might be able to find the other half of the directions."

"Well," Mr. Roberts said thoughtfully, "my parents' house is old and very large. There are probably a hundred places these papers could have been put away and forgotten. I'll phone Dan and Barbara, of course, but even if they don't know anything about it, maybe we haven't reached a dead end." He turned to Terry. "I'm sure Aunt Barbara will let you look through the house while you're staying with her this summer. And perhaps Eric and Alison can help you search, if they'd like to."

"That's a great idea!" Eric grinned..

Mr. Thorne looked doubtful, "Are you sure your sister would want two extra teenagers in her house?"

"I'll have to ask her, of course, but she loves to have young people around. She and James live in that huge place alone and he's busy with his cars and his own friends, so it's lonely for her. She can't get out much. I'm sure she'll welcome Eric and Alison along with Terry."

"What a wonderful way to spend our vacation," Alison said. "Looking for hidden treasure."

The day after school ended, Eric and Alison boarded a plane with Terry, heading for California.

"Keep this with you," Mr. Thorne told Eric just before they boarded and handed him a locked briefcase. "It has the letter and directions inside. Here's the key. I made one copy of each, but still, it wouldn't be good to have them fall into the wrong hands."

"I'll take good care of it," Eric promised.

"Good. Take care of yourselves, too."

During the plane ride, the three sipped orange juice and talked over the plans for finding the pirate's papers. Just talking about it with Terry made them more enthusiastic than ever.

"I can't wait to start looking!" he said. "I might even write a story about this someday. I want to be a writer, you know."

"But if we don't find the other half of those directions in your aunt's house," Eric asked, "will there be other places to search?"

"Sure. My uncle and aunt live in Monterey. They might have some ideas. I know we'll find it."

Their plane landed in San Francisco International Airport, and they transferred to a much smaller plane for their short flight south to Monterey. Terry's cousin James met them at the Monterey Peninsula Airport. He was a tall, heavily built man in his twenties, wearing boots, jeans, and a plaid shirt. Terry seemed glad to see him, but James didn't have much to say.

"Seems like I've been gone a year, not just a couple of months," Terry told him.

James only nodded.

"How's Aunt Barbara and Uncle Dan and Aunt Nell?"

James shrugged. "Pretty much the same."

"These are my friends, Alison and Eric Thorne."

"Hi. Here to look for buried treasure, are you?" James gave a mirthless laugh. "None around that I ever knew of."

"Then Aunt Barbara hasn't found the letter or the directions yet?" Terry looked disappointed.

"Nope. Let's pick up your baggage."

Eric and Alison followed them, Eric feeling a bit strange. "Now I wonder if we should have even come here," he said in a low voice to Alison.

"Of course we should. Just think how James will have to swallow that nasty laugh when we find it."

They retrieved their luggage, while Terry talked to James about his new life in Ivy, and James answered in monosyllables. When they had everything together, he helped them carry the suitcases to his car, a vintage blue De Soto that Eric judged to be about 1953. He whistled admiringly when he saw it. "Hey, that's a beauty!"

For the first time since they'd met him. James smiled. It was a rusty smile, as though turning up the corners of his mouth took effort. "Thanks," he mumbled. "I worked on it myself. Got it when it was nothing but a hunk of junk."

"I think you've found his soft spot," Alison whispered to Eric as they got into the back seat.

Eric knew she was right. If James hadn't talked much before, he made up for it during the ride home, describing how he'd renovated the De Soto and how he had plans to work on an old Model T Ford he'd recently bought in a junkyard.

Terry seemed to be only half listening. He looked out the window, interrupting every now and then to show them some familiar landmark. "There's the U.S. Naval Post-Graduate School over there. And the Seventeen Mile Drive isn't far. That's where the Pebble Beach golf course is. But we can't go that way today. It would take too long."

"Aren't we going to Monterey?" Eric asked as they turned south on Highway One and left that town behind.

"No, Aunt Barbara's house is down the coast, a few miles away," Terry said.

"I had to put in a new clutch, too," James was saying. "Took me three months to find one that would fit . . ."

Alison was deaf to the finer points of fixing up an old car. She gazed out the window at the waves churning against the rocky points they were passing, her eyes wide and shining. When James paused to take a breath, she pointed and asked in a hushed voice, "What's that up there?"

"Where?" Eric asked.

"You mean the house on the cliff?" Terry asked.

"Yes. The *castle* on the cliff."

"That's where we're going," Terry said. "That's Aunt Barbara's house."

As they neared it, Eric could see why Alison had called it a castle. It was three stories high, with two towers rising above its vast roof, standing alone on the grassy slope that turned to bare rock as it rose, leaning a little back as though the winds through the years had blown it into submission like the twisted cypress trees around it. Diamond-paned windows glittered in the dark stone walls and chimneys sprouted from the roof like fungus growths, green with moss. As they reached the driveway that curved around its front steps, Eric saw the massive front door opening and someone coming out.

It was a woman in a wheelchair, smiling at them, the sea breeze blowing her short, gray-brown hair. She lifted a hand to wave at them.

"There's Aunt Barbara!" Terry waved back to her.

James stopped the car and Terry leaped out to hug her. When he introduced Eric and Alison, she gave them each a smile that made them feel welcome. "You can call me Aunt Barbara too." Her voice was low-pitched, her smile warm.

"What a big house!" Alison looked around as they went inside.

"There's lots of it to take care of." Aunt Barbara wheeled her chair through the doorway and across the tiled entry hall. "Although I haven't been able to visit the upper floors for the last two years—no elevators. Now, Alison and Eric, just leave those bags inside the door and come with me. I'll show you at least part of the house so you'll know your way around."

"Which rooms will we take, Aunt Barbara?" Terry asked her. "James and I could be carrying all this stuff upstairs."

"We thought you'd like the green bedroom, same as always, and that Alison could take the south tower room and Eric the north, so they'll both have a good view." She looked at all of them. "Is that all right?"

"Fine," Terry said.

"Sounds great," Eric and Alison agreed.

"Then come along." She rolled the wheelchair a little ahead of them, down a wide corridor.

Eric still carried the locked briefcase that held the pirate's papers. For a moment he considered leaving it, but changed his mind, remembering Dad's instructions, and kept a firm hold on it as they followed Aunt Barbara.

"There are the front stairs to the upper floors," she said, pointing to a staircase leading from the hall. "The back stairs are next to the kitchen. This is my bedroom," she indicated a closed door, "and here is the room that was my father's office. We don't use half of these rooms any more since I don't have any help here. This is the game room, and here is the library."

Eric and Alison peered into the rooms as they passed them, admiring the old-fashioned furniture, the crystal and velvet, the ornate rugs and wallpapers.

"This house was built by my great-grandfather about a hundred years ago. He made a lot of money importing goods from Europe and the Orient. A lot of the things you see here were brought over. My father took over the business from him, and now my brother Dan is running it."

They saw the dining room with its heavy chairs and refectory table, and the kitchen with its open fireplace and modern appliances that Aunt Barbara said had been recently installed. Then they reached the end of the house and entered the living room.

Alison gasped and Eric, too, felt breathless. Instead of the dark, old-fashioned room they were expecting, they had walked into a chamber of light and music.

Three sides were plate glass windows, so that Eric felt suspended between the ocean and the brilliant sky. Gulls and other sea birds soared around them, their cries blending with the sound of the waves far below. Sea winds sang with soprano sounds against the glass.

"It's like another world!" Alison breathed.

"Do you like it?" Aunt Barbara smiled. "I had this room remodeled after my parents died. I would have liked to redo the whole house, but . . ." she broke off with a shrug.

"The money ran out." James appeared in the doorway and finished her sentence for her. "Everything's in the rooms, Mom."

"Thank you." Aunt Barbara gave him a look as though she hadn't liked what he'd said.

"Want me to take that briefcase you're carrying?" James asked Eric.

"No thanks. That's OK."

Aunt Barbara glanced at him. "That must be very important, Eric, the way you're holding it so tightly."

"It's the pirate's letter and half the directions. Would you like to see them?"

"I'd almost forgotten that's why you're here." She wheeled her chair to a glass-topped table. "I'd like to see them. I know they're very old so you can spread them out here, where I can see them. James, come and take a look."

Eric and Alison sat on the brightly colored, cushioned chairs and Eric unlocked the briefcase and took out the documents. Both of them waited anxiously while the others read the letter and studied the torn page, Eric hoping there would be some sign of recognition. There was none. James shook his head and silently left the room. Aunt Barbara sighed.

"I've never seen anything like these in my whole life," she said.

4 • The Search

Eric slept that night in his room in the tower, the sounds of the sea a background for his dreams. When he awoke to the clear, blue morning, he sat up to look around the room. He'd been too tired last night to really notice much more than the circular iron staircase that led to it through an opening in the center of the floor. It was a good thing he didn't walk in his sleep!

The four poster bed was against the only windowless wall. Two of the other walls had long casement windows, and the third had a large round window that overlooked the sea. He got out of bed and went to it. There was the ocean, far below, foaming toward the rocks. He smiled and turned away. This house was really something! And today they could begin searching through it for Scarab's papers! He ran down the circular stairs to wash and dress in the bathroom on the third floor. By the time he was ready, he met Alison coming along the corridor.

She was wearing jeans and sneakers, as he was, and a brown shirt that was nearly the same shade as her eyes.

"How do you like sleeping in a tower?" he asked her.

"It's different, but it's kind of scary. Hope they don't

have earthquakes here. Every time I look out that round window I feel like I'm going to fall into the ocean."

They found the staircase leading to the kitchen and went down the two flights, the scent of bacon and toast rising to meet them. Aunt Barbara was making breakfast, wheeling her chair expertly between the stove and the table, with James and Terry helping.

"Were your rooms comfortable?" she asked them.

"Fine, thanks," Eric said. "I like mine."

"So do I," Alison said. "It's like sleeping in a bird's nest, being so high up."

Aunt Barbara smiled. "I used to sleep in the south tower myself when I was a girl. I haven't even been up there for two years, ever since . . ." her smile turned bitter and her eyes sad, ". . . I've been like this."

An uncomfortable silence filled the room. James broke the silence by setting the silverware beside the plates. Terry clinked glasses as he took them out of the cupboard. Alison went to the refrigerator to get the milk.

Eric wanted to ask Aunt Barbara why she was in that wheelchair, but he didn't want to be rude. Then Alison asked. "What happened, Aunt Barbara?"

"A car accident." She changed the subject quickly. "Now, if everything's ready, I'll get the bacon and eggs. Sit down, all of you."

They took their places at the table. Eric and Alison's usually prayed before eating, though it was awkward to do sometimes in situations like this. As they did, Aunt Barbara brought a platter of food. "I suppose you're all anxious to start your search?" she asked.

"Where should we look first?" Terry asked her.

"Well, now, I've been trying to think. I suppose my father's office would be the place most papers were kept, but after he passed away, James and I went through them. We certainly didn't come across anything like that letter and torn sheet you showed us, did we, James?"

He shook his head and bit into a piece of toast.

"Maybe you should just start at the top floor of the house and work down," she went on. "You'll come across secret passages and hiding holes in this old place. Maybe some even I don't know about." She leaned forward over her plate, her tone becoming confidential. "My father was like that, you know. Enjoyed keeping things secret. And his grandfather must have been the same kind of person to have the house built that way."

Eric felt another thrill of excitement. Hidden passages! If there were all those secret places, the papers could be anywhere. "But if your father knew about Scarab's letter, he wouldn't hide it, would he? Wouldn't he want his whole family to be looking for us so they could get the other half of those directions?"

"I don't know, Eric. All he ever told Charles and Dan and me was the story of how Scarab pirated the ship and took his grandfather's jewels and money. Maybe he never knew about the letter. Maybe it was put away and lost or forgotten when this house was first built."

"Let's finish eating and get started," Terry said. "You going to help us, James?"

"Nope."

Aunt Barbara smiled indulgently. "He wouldn't take time away from working on his cars to look for a check in an envelope."

"Got customers waiting," James said.

"You mean you're going to sell that neat De Soto?" Eric asked him.

"Nope. The Jaguar I just finished." James pushed back his chair and got up. "It's in my workshop. Come around and see it if you want."

"His workshop is next to the garage," Aunt Barbara explained. "Terry can show you." And while Eric helped Alison and Terry clear the table, she told them a bit more about her son. "Never was one to bring home good grades

31

from school, but he's clever with his hands. That's where he shines. People come from as far away as Chicago just to buy one of his old cars, he does such a good job on them. Now just stack the plates here and I'll put them in the dishwasher. Run along and look for your treasure."

They climbed the steps to the third floor and then the winding staircase leading through a hole in the floor of Alison's tower bedroom. Looking around, Eric saw that her room was exactly the same as his, except for a pink comforter on the bed and green rugs instead of brown.

While he and Terry sat on the bed, Alison flung herself into a chair. "Doesn't seem there'd be any room for secret hiding places here, with all these windows. What do you think, Terry?"

"Well, one of them is a door, but it just leads out to the widow's walk." He went to one of the windows, found a handle in the frame, and pushed outward. Eric could see a narrow, railed balcony, just large enough to walk on.

"Then let's start on the floor below," he said.

They went to the playroom first, a large room with a huge fireplace. While Alison opened cupboards and chests to search them, exclaiming over the stuffed toys, dolls, and games she found there, Terry and Eric knocked on the walls and pushed at the stones of the fireplace. In half an hour they were ready to give up, but Alison, poking around the back of a deep closet, gave a cry that brought them both to see what she had found.

It was a dark recess in the back of the closet, a damp, musty smell coming from it. "I just pushed all these little desks and tables aside," Alison said, sounding thrilled. "See that dart board just above it? Well, I moved that and this panel went sliding back."

"What's in there?" Eric knelt to peer into the blackness.

Terry knelt beside him. "It just looks like a hole."

"Wish we had a flashlight."

"I'll get one," Terry offered, but Eric caught his arm.

"Not right now. I'll take a look." With a small tingle of fear he crawled forward, his hands groping. They touched cold, damp stone. But now he could see it was just a square hole with nothing in it. He pushed at the stone enclosure, but nothing moved or yielded. He crawled out again, disappointed.

"That's all there is?" Alison wailed.

Eric stood up and felt the knees of his jeans. They were dry, even though that stone floor had seemed damp. "Wonder what it's for, just an empty hole?" He pushed the dart board and watched the panel slide back again.

They explored the other rooms on the third floor—two small children's bedrooms, a larger one with a dressing room and bath, a sewing room—and found nothing more. By the time they had finished it was nearly noon. They decided to get some lunch and a flashlight before starting to search the second floor.

Neither Aunt Barbara nor James were around, but after Terry assured them it was all right to make themselves some sandwiches, they helped themselves to cheese and peanut butter from the refrigerator.

"Aunt Barbara sometimes takes a nap around this time," Terry told them, putting bread into the toaster. "Sometimes she doesn't feel so well, ever since the accident."

"What kind of accident was it?" Alison asked him.

"It was pretty awful. It happened after Grandpa died, and Grandma had something wrong with her. Aunt Barbara was driving her to the hospital and some kid on a bike went right in front of her. She tried to get out of his way and hit another car." Terry's voice was low and sorrowful. "Grandma died in the accident and Aunt Barbara's been in a wheelchair ever since."

"That's awful," Alison said quietly.

"Yeah." Terry stared at his toast, spreading peanut butter on it. He left the room for a moment and came back carrying a flashlight. "Let's take our sandwiches with us." When Eric and Alison had made their sandwiches, they were all ready to start on the second floor.

"Hope we have better luck here," Eric said as they climbed the stairs.

"What rooms are these?" Alison asked Terry.

"There's my grandparents' bedroom and the room where my grandfather kept all his collections."

"Collections?" Eric asked.

"Yeah, paintings and statues and all that kind of stuff. My dad said they were very valuable. We got part of the collection and Uncle Dan has some, and I guess Aunt Barbara has the rest."

"Let's go there first," Eric said.

"It looks like a museum!" Alison stood in the doorway.

There were glass cases, most of them empty, and tables covered with velvet cloth where statues must have been placed. On the walls were lights over faded rectangles where pictures once had hung. Only one was there now—a landscape with woods and meadows.

"Doesn't look like Aunt Barbara kept many of your family's things." Eric walked along the row of glass cases in the center of the room. One held a few china miniatures and one some small, colored glass bottles. That was all. One corner of the room held a standing suit of medieval armor and a group of crossed swords against the wall. The cases held no papers that Eric could see.

"But this would be a great place for secret passages," he said. "Let's look."

They knocked on the walls and floors again. Alison went to the suit of armor and began to examine it. "How do they make these stand up, anyway?" she asked, and when neither Terry nor Eric bothered to answer, she lifted the visor of the helmet and looked inside.

"What are you doing?" Eric asked her, worried that she might cause the whole thing to collapse.

34

"Here's the shining armor," she said with a grin. "I'm looking to see if my knight is inside."

Terry went over to her. "He'd be a mummy by now. What is in there, anyway?"

"It's so dark I can hardly see."

"Maybe he's a very short knight." Terry peered inside the open visor. "Hey, there a kind of frame in here. Let's take a look." He struggled to get the helmet loose. "Eric, give me a hand, will you?"

"What do you want to mess with that for?" Eric walked over to see. The armor was perhaps five feet tall and stood on a marble pedestal. "The papers wouldn't be in there. Or would they?"

"Can't hurt to look." Terry pulled the helmet off and they all looked inside the suit of armor.

Eric saw a metal frame that apparently held it in place. "Shine the flashlight down inside," he told Terry.

By the light they could see there were no papers in the trunk or the legs, and Alison pulled off the metal gloves to look inside them and the arms. "No papers," she said, sounding disappointed.

But Eric noticed a metal ring in the top of the frame, just inside the neck of the armor. On impulse, he stuck his index finger into the ring and pulled upward. Nothing happened.

"It isn't going to do anything," Alison told him.

Her remark made him want to prove his hunch was right. He took his finger out and tried turning the ring with his hand. It moved easily, and as he kept turning, it swung out of his grasp with a loud creaking sound. He jumped away, startled.

"Look!" Alison pointed to the floor.

The suit of armor and its pedestal had moved in an arc, and where it had been was a rectangular opening about three feet across.

Terry shone his flashlight into it. "Steps!"

Once again, Eric could smell the dampness that oozed up from this hole just as it had from the little niche in the playroom. And as they stood looking, a spider scuttled along the top step and disappeared into the darkness below.

"Should we go down?" Terry grimaced at the place the spider had been.

"Guess we'd better." Eric held out his hand to take the flashlight. "I'll go first."

Terry handed it to him. "OK, I'll follow."

"You're not leaving me behind," Alison said. "I hate spiders, but I'm not staying here while you go down there."

Eric grinned at her. "Maybe this hole's only as big as the one in the playroom. Better let me go a few steps down before you all crowd in behind me." The idea of going into that dark, dank hole was repulsive, especially since he couldn't imagine where those steps might lead.

Terry and Alison quickly agreed and stood back, away from the hole, to watch him.

Eric shined the flashlight to get a better look, but all he could see were the stone steps descending into nothingness, a few upright wooden beams around them. He took a deep breath and slid his feet down to the third step. Then, holding the flashlight in front of him, he began to descend.

5 • The Secret Passage

Dampness and a foul smell of ancient mold enveloped Eric as he went cautiously down the steep, narrow stairway. By the flashlight's glow he could see the wooden beams around him becoming solid walls.

"What's down there?" Terry's voice echoed through empty space.

"Just steps, so far." He felt very much alone in this strange place. "Come on. It seems to be OK."

He shined the flashlight on the top part of the staircase so they could see their way, and soon they stood on the steps just above him.

"Where do you think this will lead?" Alison whispered nervously.

Terry's laugh sounded nervous, too. "Don't worry. There aren't any dungeons or torture chambers."

"You sure?"

"Well, I don't think there are. But when I write my book about this, I think I'll put some in. Make it more dramatic."

"This probably leads to a hidden room." Eric said, trying to keep up his own courage. "Remember Aunt Barbara told us we'd find secret rooms and passages."

"Yeah," Terry said. "We should have asked her if she'd been in any of them."

"Sure smells awful." Alison sniffed the air.

"Hold on to my hand," Terry told her. "I'll help you down these steps."

Eric groaned inwardly. Was Terry just trying to be helpful, or was he getting mushy over Alison? He hoped not, when there was a fortune in gold and jewels waiting to be found and no time to waste. He turned abruptly and began his descent once more.

In a few minutes the stairs ended and became a passage leading off to the right. It was narrow, and so low he had to bend his six-foot frame to get through. He kept the beam of the flashlight on the floor well ahead of him, so he'd be sure to see any hole or sudden drop.

The smell of moldy stone faded in a thick aroma of dust and old wood.

"I bet we're on the first floor," Terry whispered behind him. "Stop here a minute. Maybe this passage opens into one of the rooms down here."

"What if it does?" Alison asked. "We're looking for hiding places, not rooms."

"That's exactly it," Terry said. "We could find false walls with storage places inside them, or secret closets. Anything. Here, Eric, shine the light along the wall."

While Eric directed the flashlight on the wall as they walked, Terry thumped in several places. In a few moments one of his thumps produced a hollow sound. There, set horizontally in the wall close to the floor, was a metal pull handle. Eric bent to take a good look at it. It was half eaten with rust. He pulled outward, but nothing happened. Pushing in brought the same result.

"Look." Alison picked up the light that Eric had set on the floor and shone it on the wall to either side of the handle. "See those cracks? Try pulling up on the handle."

The cracks were long and straight, going halfway up the

wall about three feet apart, as though marking off a section. He lifted and heard the creaking of levers as the panel slid upward. Now a strip of sunlight shone into the darkness where they stood, and a row of books could be see just inside the opening.

"It comes out in a bookcase." Terry bent and pushed at the books to clear a path. "They're on a sort of tray so you can push them all sideways at once."

"Whoever built all these things was a genius at mechanics," Eric said. "He could just crawl through the bookcase and set the books in place again by moving the tray from here."

Terry went through first, and Eric let Alison go ahead of him. Soon they were all in a bright room filled with filing cabinets, shelves of books and papers, a desk, and in one corner a couch and chair covered with some kind of rich, embroidered fabric that looked like an oriental rug.

"It's Grandpa's office," Terry said. "I wonder if he knew about the passage?"

"He must have," Alison said. "If he took out one of those books on the tray, he'd see it, wouldn't he? So would anyone who came here to dust."

Eric slid the tray back into place. It ran smoothly along the wooden surface of the bookcase's lower shelf. He pulled out a book and saw that the tray was exactly the same color and grain as the shelf, and stayed firmly in place. "Maybe not," he said as he replaced the book. "The tray doesn't move unless you force it sideways. That's a neat piece of work!" He stood up and looked around.

"Aunt Barbara said she'd looked through all the papers in here," Terry said. "Let's go on. I want to see where else we end up."

Crawling through the bookcase again, they went back into the dark passage and closed the wall panel after them.

"Now I know how a mole must feel," Alison said

wistfully. "You just start to get warm in the sunlight and then you have to crawl back into your dark little hole again."

"We're not trying to get a California suntan," Eric said as they went along the passage. "We're looking for treasure, remember?" He felt impatient with her, and anxious to get on with the search. Visions of a chest overflowing with gold and diamonds and pearls hovered at the back of his mind.

"Getting gold fever, Eric?" Alison laughed, and Eric's vision dissolved.

"No way," he muttered, but maybe she was right. He'd better watch himself. The treasure was family heirlooms, after all, and not a vast cache of wealth for him to spend. What had he been thinking, anyway?

Now, by the light of the flashlight, he saw there were more steps ahead of them. "We're going down again," he warned the others. "Watch your step."

Terry raised his voice. "We're now approaching the bargain basement, Ladies . . . I mean Lady and Gentleman. Here you will see the hot water heater, the central heating system, and the termites."

Alison giggled. "Really?"

"Well, I'm pretty sure these stairs are going past the basement now."

"Then this house must have a sub-basement," Eric said. And that was strange. It was built on what had looked like solid rock.

"If the papers are hidden down here," Alison said, "I hope they're in something waterproof."

That was true. Eric could feel a breeze that smelled like the ocean. He slowed his steps, hoping the flashlight's batteries would hold out, wondering if there would be a hidden pool somewhere along the way. In fact, he could hear the sound of water splashing, faint but clear, and was that a glow in the distance? "I think we're near the end of

40

the tunnel," he told the others. "Be careful. These stones are getting slippery."

The sounds of splashing water grew louder as they went. Soon they were far below the basement, and the irregular opening where the faint light glowed was only a few feet ahead of them. When they reached it, they found it was wide enough for them to stand together, and they all looked out at a vast cave. The ocean flowed about ten feet below them, lapping at shelves of rock, ebbing and then rolling in again to stream in little channels under and between the rocks. The stone ceiling of the cave was hung with stalactites like grotesque icicles. A cool sea wind swept around them, and from here Eric could see the mouth of the cave about a hundred feet away to the right, where sunlight glittered on the waves as they washed in.

An ancient metal ladder hung at the lip of the opening where they stood and extended down to a broad ledge of rock that ran along the side of the cave. Across the water, on the other side, were dark openings. Eric couldn't see what they were in this dim light, but he could make out a small boat that rode on the swell, its wooden hull eaten away by time and the sea so that it looked like a skeleton ship anchored on the tide.

"Man!" Terry breathed beside him.

"Do we have to go in there?" Alison looked around the cave.

"Did you know this cave was under the house?" Eric asked Terry.

"No. I never knew there was anything like this!" Terry frowned. "That boat must have been here for years. There's nowhere on shore to launch a boat—it's too rocky around here. Maybe Grandpa or somebody found this place and used it to keep a boat in."

"But then why the secret passage?" Eric leaned against the walls of the house.

"If all they wanted was to go boating," Alison said, "they

wouldn't have gone to so much trouble. They'd have just built a passage to the basement and gotten into the house from there."

"But this tunnel opens into your grandfather's office, Terry, and then it goes up to that collection room on the second floor," Eric pointed out. "Somebody wanted to get from here to those rooms without being seen."

Terry scratched his head, looking mystified.

"Let's go," Alison said impatiently. "It's cold and damp and scary down here. I don't want to stand around talking."

"Then let's look for the pirate's papers," Eric said. "Maybe they're in the cave somewhere."

"You really think they could be down *there?*" She gripped the edge of the opening tightly as she looked out.

"We'll have to take a look," Eric said. "See what's on these ledges of rock, and look in that old wrecked boat."

"And across the water, there," Terry pointed. "Those look like little caves. We should search them, too."

"Wait a minute!" Alison said indignantly. "I'm not swimming across the water to search those caves."

"It isn't far across," Terry said.

"But I don't have my swimsuit!" She looked from Terry to Eric. "You two can go if you want, but I'm not swimming in my jeans. And anyway, I don't want to go at all. This cave is creepy."

"Then Terry and I can go," Eric said. "OK, Terry?"

"Sure."

"While we're gone, you can search this side of the cave, Alison."

"Maybe this is high tide. If we wait for low tide, we might be able to walk across to the caves," Alison suggested.

"But low tide might not be for hours yet." Eric stuck his head out the opening and tried to see the end of the cavern, searching for a stretch of rock they might walk across. All he could see was several channels full of water. "For all we know, *this* could be low tide," he said. "I think we'd better start swimming."

He pushed the flashlight through the belt of his jeans, swung outside the opening, and set his feet firmly on the metal rungs of the ladder. Chill air moved around him, and he could feel the rust from the ladder on his hands. He hoped the rungs wouldn't break; they were badly eroded. But they held his weight until he reached bottom. He looked up to see Terry halfway down and Alison just above him. Good. He knew she wouldn't back out. He turned to look around the cave from this vantage point.

She was right. It was creepy, full of shadows and strange, hollow noises from its rocky depths.

And then a sound rose from somewhere below . . . the sound of a voice raised in a sad cry that echoed and re-echoed around them.

6 • A Cry in the Cavern

Eric felt goosepimples prickling his skin as the cry came again. Beside him, Alison and Terry stood motionless. Then he heard his sister's words, quiet and quavering.

"What's that?"

He shook his head, his voice frozen in his throat. The sound was coming from below them, under their ledge where the water foamed into the cave from the sea. Heart pounding, he knelt and leaned over the edge to see.

"Let's get out of here!" Alison spoke in a hoarse whisper, but she, too, squatted beside Eric and tried to see under the ledge.

"The flashlight," Terry said. "Shine it down there."

Eric had forgotten it. Now he pulled it from his belt and flicked it on. At the same time he heard a loud splash, and a dark shape appeared just under the surface of the water. He followed it with the light. The shape moved in a swift arc, then disappeared under the rolling waves.

"It's a seal," said Terry, sounding relieved.

"But it sounded so human!" Alison stood up. "Let's go."

"Yeah. Come on." Terry got up and moved for the ladder. Eric followed them, still feeling a chill of fear. It was

44

just some sea creature, but here in this dim cave it had set his nerves tingling. The last thing he wanted to do now was swim across that stretch of water where the dark shape had disappeared. He reached the top of the ladder, where the other two waited.

"Can I have the flashlight?" Alison asked. "I want to walk ahead on the way back. Then I'll know it's you two behind me and not something even more horrible."

Eric gave her the light and let her and Terry precede him back along the passage, thinking that the experience hadn't damaged Alison's sense of humor, such as it was. He felt a lot better now, too, as they climbed the stairway, even though the air was just as foul as it had been. "Let's go through the bookcase in the office," he called to them.

It wasn't hard to find the handle to the secret panel again, and soon they were all in the office, taking deep breaths of fresh air from the partly opened window.

Alison sat down on the couch, while Terry took the chair beside it and Eric stretched out on the floor.

"You're covered with dust," Alison told him, laughing.

"So are you two, and you're getting it on the furniture." Eric looked at the dust and cobwebs in her hair, and her smudged face.

"So what do we do now?" Terry asked. "We've got to find some way to look around down there."

"And quick," Eric said. "If we waste much more time, somebody else could find that treasure."

Alison gave him a quizzical look. "That's a weird thing to say, Eric. It's been there for a hundred years. A few more days won't make any difference. Besides, how could anyone else find it without the directions?"

"I know. I just want to hurry up and find it." How could he explain this urgent feeling he had?

Terry glanced at his watch. "It's after five o'clock," he said. "I think we ought to shower and get ready for dinner. Then we can tell Aunt Barbara and James about the cave.

Maybe they know something about it, or about this passage."

When Eric had washed and changed into clean white cords and a white knit shirt, he went downstairs to the kitchen. Terry was the only one there, getting a glass of water.

"Come on into the living room," he said. "My Aunt Nell and Uncle Dan are here."

"Did you tell them what we found today?"

"No. We were waiting for you."

In the glass-walled room, Terry introduced his uncle, a tall, thin man with a large nose and a good-humored expression. Aunt Nell was nearly as tall as her husband and wore her long, coffee-colored hair tied back with a shell comb. She wore a bright yellow blouse with an orange skirt, and Eric thought her beautiful. Alison was already here, neat and pretty in a pink dress, and James was standing behind his mother's wheelchair, looking uncomfortable in dark slacks and a white shirt with a red tie.

"I'm glad you're here, Eric," Aunt Barbara smiled. "Now you can tell us about your adventures today. Did you find the pirate's papers?"

"Not yet." Eric seated himself in the circle the group had formed around the coffee table. "But we did find a secret passage."

With Alison and Terry joining in, he told them about the secret passage, the vast cave, and the old boat. Alison told them about the strange cry they'd heard.

Aunt Barbara and Dan exchanged amused glances.

"Sea lions," Dan said.

But James looked surprised. "You know about this cave, Mom?"

46

She turned her head to look up at him. "Yes, James. I even went there once many years ago."

"But why didn't you tell me about it?" He looked hurt.

"Tell you?" She turned her head away from him and Eric could see regret on her face. She looked down at her fingers as they plucked nervously at the pleats of her print dress. "I'm sorry. I guess I just never thought about it. I've had so many things on my mind. I didn't even remember that cave until just now."

Dan spoke heartily. "We found out about it when we were kids, James, and that was a very long time ago."

"Oh, it wasn't *that* long ago." Nell took his hand and smiled at him. "But you never told me about it, either, Dan."

"Well, it isn't the sort of thing you go around telling people." He gave them all a sheepish smile. "Seems one of our ancestors ran a smuggling business on the side. Ships brought art objects from Europe, oriental rugs, that kind of thing, all duty free since the government didn't know about it. He got rich from it too."

"Was he the one who built this house?" Eric asked eagerly.

"That's the one. He must have built those secret passages at the same time. We found them long ago and went down to the cave, but Terry's father, Barbara, and I weren't adventurous enough to go farther. We thought it was a gloomy place. We climbed down the ladder and saw some sea lions, and then we went right back up it again."

"That's what we did," Alison laughed. "Only we didn't know that thing was a sea lion."

"Yes we did," Terry said, embarrassed.

"So you never explored those caves?" Eric asked Dan.

"I never went back down there. Just didn't care to. Did you, Barbara?"

"No, and I'm sure Charles didn't either. It frightened me, I remember. All those weird sounds and shadows."

"I think it's awesome," Terry said. "When I write my book about this I'm going to describe the cave. You should go down and take a look, James."

"Got better things to do," James muttered.

Aunt Barbara looked guilty. "Yes, he has. He has a crippled mother to look after, and cars to work on so he can support the two of us."

"Now, Barbara," Dan said heartily, "you know Nell and I are here to help any time you need us. Right now I'm anxious to hear more about this hidden treasure." He turned to Eric. "Charles and Barbara told me about the pirate's letter and that half page of directions. Could we see the ones you have?"

"Sure. I'll go get them." Eric went upstairs to get the briefcase, glad to leave the room. He found himself liking James a lot better now than he had when they'd first met. As soon as Eric had some time he'd go take a look at those cars. He got the briefcase and brought it back to the living room.

Alison and Nell were helping Aunt Barbara carry in plates of chicken salad and rolls, while James and Terry set silverware on the glass-topped table. Eric was relieved to see Aunt Barbara looking cheerful again.

"We're going to eat dinner in here," she told him. "You go ahead and show Dan and Nell those papers while we get everything ready."

Dan studied the letter first, then passed it to Nell while he looked at the torn page in its leather frame. "I never knew anything like these existed," he said. "Our family was supposed to get them, too, right? Wonder why we never heard anything about them?"

"That's the burning question," Aunt Barbara said. "I can only guess that Grandfather or someone put them away and forgot about them. The food's all ready, so come sit at the table."

"Do you know anything about the old fort Scarab

mentioned, Mr. Roberts?" Eric asked while they were eating. "Or a rock shaped like a lion's head?"

"Well, what is now the Presidio in Monterey was a fort back in Scarab's time. The Spanish built El Castillo there in 1793, and when California became a state, Commodore Sloat built Fort Mervine in 1846."

Eric felt a sudden thrill of elation. "Then that must be it! And there's a road going south that leads to a boulder that's shaped like a lion's head. That's pretty clear."

"But I don't know of any boulder like that." Dan looked at his wife. "Do you, Nell?"

"No," she said hesitantly. "At least I can't think of it right at the moment. But it almost seems that I've seen one . . ."

"You *have?*" Eric noticed everyone staring at him and realized he'd shouted. He lowered his voice with an effort, trying to keep his excitement in check. "Could you possibly remember where it is?"

"Please try, Aunt Nell," Terry said.

"I *am* trying, dear, but I just can't seem to recall right now." She closed her eyes and passed a slender hand across her forehead.

"Nell knows this coast very well," Aunt Barbara told Eric and Alison. "She's painted pictures of most of it."

"She's good, too," Terry said.

"Thank you." Nell smiled at them. "But I'm afraid I can't remember that rock. I might have seen something like it somewhere, but it just won't come to me. Maybe it will, later."

Eric was disappointed. "But anyway, we know where the fort is. And if we follow the road south from the fort, we might run across the lion's head rock ourselves."

"Well," Uncle Dan said, "the Presidio itself was moved to where it is now in the early 1900's. And all that's left of Fort Mervine is a few cannons and some earthen walls covered with grass. I think whatever roads were there when Scarab wrote his directions must be gone by now."

"You're going to need the other half of those directions," Aunt Barbara said.

James turned his rusty smile to Eric. "If the fort's gone, the road's gone, and there's no rock, how do you think you guys are going to find the treasure?"

"You don't really believe there is one, do you?" Eric asked him.

James shook his head. "Pipe dreams."

"But you've seen the letter and the directions." Eric wished James wouldn't be so pessimistic about it, when he and the others were so sure they'd find it. "And you know the story about Scarab robbing our ancestors."

Dan smiled at James. "You'd make a good scientist. You don't believe in anything you can't see and touch. Right?"

"Not exactly. I believe what I believe. The pirate's letter is real enough. But a treasure lying around for a hundred years? . . ." he broke off with a skeptical look and shrugged. "No way."

Eric glanced from Alison to Terry, discouraged. Maybe the papers weren't even here. And even if they did find them, someone could have already taken the treasure.

Suddenly this whole idea seemed to be just what James had called it. A pipe dream.

7 • A New Plan

Next morning, after they'd helped Aunt Barbara clean up the breakfast dishes and tidy the kitchen, Eric asked Terry and Alison to go outside with him. "I want to take a look at the cliff out behind the house, and try to see the entrance of the cave from there," he told them.

"Why?" Terry looked puzzled.

"I have an idea," Eric said.

Terry led the way around the house and up a rocky slope until they stood at the very edge of the cliff. They had to get down on their stomachs to peer over the rim.

"Can you see anything?" Alison asked. "This is making me dizzy." She sat up, away from the cliff edge.

Eric looked down at the sun-silvered water spotted with dark patches of seaweed. "The entrance is hidden from here," he said. "It must be pretty well hidden from any ships that pass this way, too. All those rocks." The bottom of the cliff was a maze of jagged brown rocks where the waves churned into white lace.

"What's your idea?" Terry sat up too, and looked curiously at him.

"I'm not sure it's any good," Eric said. "Maybe James is

right. Maybe this is all stupid, searching for that treasure."

"Eric, I don't know what's got into you." Alison gave him
a baffled look. "First you can't wait to find the treasure,
and now you're so down about it."

She's right, Eric thought. Ever since he'd heard about
the treasure he'd been feeling . . . different. It was hard to
put into words, but he could tell there was something
funny going on inside him. "Well," he said, "how do you
guys feel about it? Want to keep on searching?"

Terry hooted. "If you quit, Alison and I will keep on,
won't we, Alison?"

"Of course. Don't let what James thinks get you down,
Eric. He seems to be pessimistic about everything."

"OK." He grinned at them, feeling better. "Here's my
idea. If we could get a boat somewhere, we could get into
the cave that way."

"Uncle Dan has one," Terry said. "He might let us borrow it. That would be a lot easier than swimming to the
other side of the cave."

"Sure would," Eric said.

"I'll go phone him right now." Terry jumped up and ran
down the rocky slope.

"Why don't we just search the rest of the house first?"
Alison asked. "We haven't finished the second floor or the
first floor or the basement, yet."

Eric pushed himself back from the cliff edge, rolled over
and closed his eyes in the warmth of the sun. "I think you
just don't want to back down in the cave, Allie."

"You're right."

"But the cave is the best place to look. If there was
smuggling going on, there's probably lots of stuff hidden
away down there."

"Maybe there's lots of stuff hidden in the house."

"But the Roberts family would have found them by
now." He propped his head on his hand and idly flipped a

pebble over the cliff edge. "They all knew about the secret passage, didn't they?"

"All except James," Alison said. "So?"

"Think about it. Don't you know every place in our house?"

"Sure. We used to go exploring the basement and the attic and everywhere when we were little." She nodded. "I see what you mean. Kids get into everything."

"Right. So they would have found those papers by now, if they were anywhere in the house."

"Not necessarily. What kid would pay attention to some old papers? They'd probably crayon all over them."

Eric scratched at his nose. "Well, maybe. In that case, we won't be able to use them anyway."

"Why do you think they never told James?"

"I figured Aunt Barbara lived here when she was a kid, then she got married and left and had James. She didn't come back until her father died, a couple of years ago. By then, James was grown up and interested in his vintage cars. Like she said, I think she just plain forgot about it, with the accident and her parents dying and everything."

"Hey!" Terry was calling to them. Eric sat up and saw him standing under a cypress, waving to them.

"Come on! It's OK!"

Eric helped Alison to her feet and they ran down the slope.

"Uncle Dan was at work," Terry said as they approached. "But Aunt Nell says we can borrow the boat if we're careful with it. She's home now and she'll let us have it right away."

"Is it a sailboat?" Eric asked.

"No, it's a motor launch. A small one. They use it for fishing and water skiing." He led the way around the garage. "Let's ask James if he'll drive us into Monterey."

Eric's good spirits vanished. "I bet he won't take us."

"Sure he will," Terry grinned. "We'll just tell him we'd like a ride in that Studebaker he's fixing up."

James's workshop was a large shed connected to the garage by a door in the wall. A Model A Ford body, rusted to a rich orange, sat on blocks on the driveway outside, and an ancient Studebaker was just inside the wide entrance. Eric looked at the assortment of fenders, bumpers and various engine parts, and let out an admiring whistle. "Man! Look at this stuff!"

James was working under the Studebaker, lying on a wheeled dolly. He rolled himself out and looked up at them. "Hi."

"Hi." Eric patted the car's fender. "This is a real antique."

James sat up and wiped the back of one greasy hand across his oil-stained cheek. "Sure. Did you notice the airplane nose?"

Eric nodded. "It's neat. Are you finished with it?"

"No. It's got a leak in the trans. Just trying to find it."

"It sure looks great." Eric eyed the shining gray body and the immaculate interior.

A white smile appeared on the blackened face. "Thanks."

"Could we go for a ride in it?" Terry asked.

"Not until I fix the leak."

Alison looked really disappointed. "I've always wanted to ride in a rumble seat."

The white smile grew broader. "Studebakers don't have rumble seats. I've got a convertible, though. A '51 Cadillac. It's in the garage. I don't have a top for it yet, but we can take a spin in it if you like."

"I'd love it." She smiled back at him.

"OK. Wait till I take off my coveralls and wash up." He removed his oil-stained cap and placed it on the dolly. "Aren't you guys searching for treasure today?"

Terry leaned against the Studebaker's door. "Yeah.

54

Actually, James, we want you to drive up to Uncle Dan's so we can borrow his boat. We're going to get into the underground cave that way. Do you mind?"

"Naw. Got to give that Cad a test drive, anyhow." He went into a small bathroom and closed the door.

Terry and Eric poked around the workshop while they waited, examining the tools and exclaiming over the assortment of hubcaps that decorated one wall.

"Look at this," Alison said after a few minutes, and held up a framed picture she'd found on a small desk in the corner.

Eric and Terry went to see. The picture showed a tall, good-looking woman standing next to a dark haired man with a mustache. Both were on skis, and there were snow-covered trees in the background.

"That's Aunt Barbara," Terry said. "And that must be Uncle Paul. I can hardly remember him. He died when I was small."

"She looks so young," Alison said, "I hardly recognized her."

Terry nodded. "She liked to ski. Won all sorts of prizes. She used to water ski, too."

In a few minutes James was ready, and took them into the garage. The Cadillac was black with white leather seats. Eric noticed the De Soto parked beside it, and a white Jaguar beyond that. It would be great to have a sportscar like the Jag, he thought as he climbed into the back seat with Alison. Maybe when they found the treasure, he could buy himself one. Even if he had to share it with Alison, it would be great. He leaned his head against the back of the seat and watched a line of white and brown birds—pelicans?—gliding over the sea. That treasure was around here somewhere. He would find it. He wouldn't quit, no matter how discouraged he got.

By the time James had reached the highway, Eric was

so lost in his dreams of the treasure, he didn't know Alison was talking to him until she jabbed him in the ribs.

"Eric!"

"Uh . . . oh . . . what?" He blinked at her.

"I said, should we stop at a florist and have him send some flowers to Aunt Barbara? You know, as a sort of 'thank you for having us' present?"

"Yeah. That's a good idea."

"Were you falling asleep?"

"No. Just daydreaming, I guess." He sat up and watched the deserted coastline. "This is really pretty, isn't it?" He hoped Alison hadn't guessed his thoughts, as she sometimes did.

When they arrived in Monterey, James obligingly stopped at the florist's, where they ordered an arrangement of pink and red carnations to be delivered to Aunt Barbara.

Then they drove on to the house where Nell and Dan lived. It was at the end of a quiet, pretty street where flowers bloomed around every house and magnolia trees shaded the sidewalk.

Nell, looking fresh and attractive in a lavender sun dress, took them out to the garden that led to a little dock and a small private beach.

"There's our boat," she said, pointing to a sleek motor launch moored at the dock. "Now, would you all like some cake and lemonade before you take off?"

"No thanks," Eric said quickly, although he would have enjoyed staying longer with her in this sunlit garden. "We have to search that cave today, and it's a big place. By the way," Eric asked Nell, "did you remember anything more about the lion's head rock?"

"No. I just can't seem to recall. But I think Dan has some information that might interest you. He knows a lot about the history of Monterey, and last night on the way home, he remembered reading about a pirate who lived here years ago."

"We already knew that," Alison said. "After Scarab gave up pirating, he settled here."

Nell frowned thoughtfully. "No, that wasn't the name Dan remembered."

"Scarab was only a nickname," Eric said.

"Well, then, Dan can tell you the name of the pirate and where he's buried."

"Somewhere around here?" Terry asked.

"Yes. Dan is going to find out just where today. He'll let you know."

They thanked her, but Eric didn't think the information would be of much help to them, although the didn't say so. It would have been great if she'd been able to tell them where the lion's head rock was.

Nell turned her attention to James. "How about something to eat before you have to drive back?" she asked him.

"No thanks. Got to pick up some things at the auto supply."

"All right, then," she said. "Terry, you know how to run the boat, don't you? Please, all of you, be careful and don't take unnecessary risks in that cave. We'll all be anxious to hear what you find there."

Alison smiled at James before they got into the boat. "It was really a neat ride over here," she said, "even if you didn't have a rumble seat."

8 • The Caves

The boat ride back took much longer than the drive with James. They had to go around the peninsula, past the town of Pacific Grove with its white beaches and cliffs blooming with colorful ice plants. Terry kept the boat as close as he could to the rugged shoreline so they could admire the view.

"Monarch butterflies spend the winters here," he told them. "They cluster all over some of the trees."

Farther on, he pointed out the white dunes of Asilomar State Beach and showed them where the Seventeen Mile Drive followed the rocky coast. Eric watched the crashing surf and saw the twisted cypress trees above it, wondering if the pirate's treasure could be hidden there. In spite of the coast's wild beauty, he was glad when they left it and sped across the open ocean once more, past Carmel Bay and Point Lobos.

It was after noon when he could see Aunt Barbara's towered house on its cliff, and when they were near it, Terry slowed the boat. "Got to be careful here," he said. "That surf looks heavy."

Eric studied the rocks, trying to find the mouth of the

cave, not seeing it. There was only a solid parade of rocks looming jaggedly along the bottom of the cliff. "Can you see the entrance?" he asked the others.

Alison shook her head, her hair whipping like a dark cloud in the breeze.

"There has to be a way in there," Terry said, frowning.

Then Eric remembered. When they'd looked over the cliff this morning, he'd seen that some of the rocks were like little islands standing out in the sea. From here, you couldn't tell that. They looked as though they ran straight across the bottom of the cliff. Whether it was some trick of light or the reflections of the sea, he couldn't tell. "I think if we go slowly toward that high rock right there," he told the others, "we'll be able to see the cave mouth."

Terry guided the craft as close to the rock as he could. It stood alone, a few yards from the shore. In a moment they had rounded it, and there was the cave entrance directly ahead of them. They all gave whoops of victory until the little boat was gliding into the cavern, leaving the sunlight behind.

Something moved on the rocky ledge to their left, and Eric saw two dark bodies gleaming in the dimness. Sea lions. The creatures peered at them with round, inquisitive eyes, then dove into the water, yelping their fear. Their cries echoed through the cave and the boat rocked as they swam past it to the open sea outside.

Alison laughed nervously. "Well, at least we were expecting them this time."

"Wonder if there's anything else here?" Eric looked around at the vast expanse of the cavern, full of shadows.

Terry cut the motor and the boat bobbed quietly on the swell. "Here," he said, handing Eric one of two paddles he'd fished from under his seat. "We have to use these, now. Which side do we search first?"

To their left Eric could see the ledge where they'd come down the metal ladder yesterday. To their right, the rotting boat was secured to a wooden dock supported by pilings. "This must be where the smugglers unloaded their goods. Maybe they stored stuff in those caves." He pointed to the two openings in the rock they'd seen yesterday. Now he could see they were natural formations, probably carved by the ancient seas that once covered this land. The irregular holes were large enough for several people to pass through, but from here he couldn't tell what lay inside the dark interiors. "Let's go into those, first," he said.

They paddled the few strokes to the wooden dock, finding several metal rings set along its length. Terry got out and moored the boat to one of them.

"They must have tied several boats here at one time," Eric said, keeping his voice low. Everything echoed interminably here so that the water coursing through the channels sounded like rapids, and the sloshing waves seemed to crash.

Terry looked at the skeleton ship. "There's not enough of this old thing to search. It's so rotten we couldn't even board her."

Eric and Alison scrambled up on the dock.

"I'm bringing the flashlight from the boat," she said. "Did you guys remember to bring one?"

"I did." Terry showed her the light fastened to the belt of his jeans by a metal clip.

Eric headed for the opening closest to the mouth of the cave, the others following. "Might as well start here and work our way around as much of this place as we can."

"Sure. That's a peachy idea," Alison said grimly. She shined her flashlight on the floor just inside the opening.

Eric noticed a strong, unfamiliar scent as he stepped into the cave. Terry was right beside him and was shining his light on a heap of something near the wall.

"Hey, look at this. Wooden slats. Bet this used to be a packing crate."

60

"See anything else?" Eric moved away from Terry toward another pile.

"I'm looking." Terry and his light moved around the cave wall.

"Alison, bring your light over here, will you?" Eric called.

She came hesitantly inside, to where Eric stood.

They could hear a sound overhead. Something in the cave with them, a whirring, squeaking, fluttering turmoil.

"What's that?" Alison pointed her light upward.

Bats—hundreds of them, hanging in clusters among the stalactites—roused now by the light so that before anyone could move they were surrounded by dozens of frantic, leathery wings and hurtling furry bodies.

Eric tried to beat them away from his face, but they battered him, blindly flapping against him.

Alison screamed. Terry shouted with fear.

"My hair!" Alison shrieked. "They're in my hair!"

Eric held his arms over his face and forced his way through the rain of bodies, trying to reach her. After what seemed endless time he could see her through the whirling mass. She was crouched on the floor in the beam of the fallen flashlight, hands over her face, bats whipping around and against her, one caught in strands of her hair, yanking them upward in a blind attempt to free itself. Eric swatted at it, and it fell against her neck before it rose again, squeaking and flapping.

Eric moved in close to her, until finally he had her head in his arms, protecting it, huddling his own head down over hers.

The squeaking, fluttering noises subsided. The turmoil lessened, slowly, until at last there was just an occasional sound of flight above them. They crouched together until he could hear only the tinkling of water, the washing of waves, and the distant echoes outside the cave. Then, slowly, he lifted his head.

The darkness above them was still. Alison clung to him, sobbing faintly.

"You OK now?" he asked her.

She made a sound that was no more than a sigh.

Eric stretched out his hand, weakly, to take the still burning flashlight. He shone it toward the cave wall, where he'd last seen Terry. There he was, kneeling, face to the wall, arms protecting his head. As the light flashed near him he lowered his arms slowly, turned his head, and blinked.

"You all right?" Eric asked him.

"I . . . I think so." He got cautiously to his feet, using the wall for support, then turned and came toward Eric. "Are they all gone?"

"Yeah. They all flew out." He played the beam of light on the ceiling so they could see that only stalactites remained there, gleaming dully.

"What happened?" Terry sounded worried.

Eric moved his other arm down to her shoulder and peered at her head. "You didn't get bitten, did you?"

She kept her hands over her face and gave a sob. He could feel her shaking. By the light, he could see that her hands bore several scratch marks. He had the same marks on his own hands.

"I got scratched, too," Terry said, "but no bites."

"Me neither," Eric said. "Alison, how about you?"

Slowly she moved her hands from her face as though with great effort. Her eyes were wide and frightened. Tears coursed down her cheeks. "That was horrible," she said in a quivering voice. "Horrible."

"But you didn't get bitten?" Eric insisted.

"No. I don't think so. I didn't feel any bites. Just those awful beating wings and claws." She shivered and sighed.

"One of them got tangled up in her hair," Eric told Terry. "That's what scared her so badly."

"Yuk!" Terry held out his hands toward her. "Here. You

can get up now. Nothing's going to hurt you any more. They're all gone."

She stretched her hands tentatively out toward his and he pulled her gently to her feet.

Eric shone the beam of the flashlight on the floor as they went toward the opening, staying on one side of Alison while Terry stayed on the other. There were a few dead bats lying among heaps of wood and other debris, but if Alison saw them, she said nothing. In a moment they were once again standing on the dock.

Eric looked at his sister, her face pale and drawn in the dimness. He knew she'd been badly frightened, they all had, but already he was feeling that familiar urgency. The directions to the treasure was here somewhere. He didn't want any more delay. He wanted to find them.

"Feeling better now?" he asked her.

"A little."

"Think you can go on?"

"Go on where?" She looked up at him.

"Go on searching the rest of this place."

"Have you lost your marbles, Eric Thorne?"

"Hey, they were only bats. They didn't hurt us."

"No? How would you like to have one in *your* hair?"

"I got it out, didn't I?" Eric felt much better. Alison sounded normal now.

"It felt like you were trying to pull my hair out by the roots!"

"Well, how else could I get the bats out of your belfry?"

Terry snorted.

Alison turned on him. "He's not so funny."

"My flashlight," Terry mumbled. "I left it in the cave. I'll just slip back and get it, if you'll give me yours for a sec, Eric."

"Sure." Eric handed him the flashlight.

"I'm going back to the house," Alison said firmly. "You're crazy if you think I'm staying here one more minute."

"OK. Terry and I will go on searching."

"Yeah? Well, suppose there's more of those things in the next cave?"

"This time," Eric said, "we'll be smart enough to look first. I should have known. That awful smell in there was bat droppings."

"They could be rabid. They could have bitten us." She was furious. "They might even be around here someplace now."

"I'm pretty sure they'd all fly out the mouth of the cave. They have to go outside every night to look for food, you know. And they probably only live in the cave nearest the outside, anyway, so they'd be able to fly in and out easily."

"When did you become an authority on bats?"

"I've read a little," he said. "Look, if I promise to go into every place first and look around, will you stay with us until we search the rest of these caves?"

"Maybe Terry wants to go back to the house, too."

"Sure I do," Terry said coming back toward them. "This place doesn't really turn me on. But since we went to all the trouble of getting the boat and everything . . ."

"Then I'm going back alone," Alison said.

"OK, OK." Eric took the flashlight Terry handed him. "Let's ferry her across to the passageway, Terry."

"We'd all have to go," Eric said. "How could we search here without a flashlight?"

"Well," Terry said, "we could take the boat back to Aunt Nell's and drop you off there, Alison."

"But then I'd have to ask Nell or somebody to drive me back here while you two brought the boat back again. By then it would be dark, wouldn't it?" She glanced across the frothing water toward the entrance to the passage, then smiled faintly. "Any way you look at it, we'd have to put the search off, and I want to find Scarab's papers as much as you do."

"I guess we're all in this together, aren't we?" She sighed. "OK, let's get on with the search. But if I see one more bat . . ."

"I promised we'd watch out for them, didn't I?" Eric grinned at her, relieved.

At the entrance of the next cave, they shone the flashlight beam around the ceiling and walls.

"No bats," Terry said.

"Nothing much else, either," Alison said. "Just the same mess we saw in the first cave."

Eric looked around at the wooden crates and barrels rotting in the dampness, then played the light toward the back of the cave. It was smaller than the first, with the ceiling and walls almost meeting at its end. Over the litter of wood, filthy canvas, and debris, Eric could see a rectangular object. A thrill went through him. "Look!"

"Is it a chest?" Terry leaned forward.

"I think so." Alison sounded excited. "Let's take a look."

As eager as Eric was, he moved slowly, lighting their way as they stepped over piles of rubble and around fallen barrels toward the back of the cave. As they went, they heard scurrying noises echoing around them. Rats or mice, Eric thought. He wondered if Alison would want to turn back, but her footsteps never faltered as she walked beside him.

The object was indeed a chest—black, bound with strips of eroded metal, and fastened shut with an ancient lock. Excitement made his heart pound as Eric fell to his knees beside it and tugged at the lock. It held securely.

Terry and Alison were examining the top and sides.

"It's just wood," Terry said. "Painted wood—and half rotted through."

"We can just break through the top of it," Alison suggested. "Those metal bands are the only things holding it together."

Terry kicked at the side. There was a cracking sound,

and the wood caved in slightly. He surveyed the dent he'd made, then kicked it again.

The rotting wood was giving, but Eric had to get the blade of his knife into the crack Terry had made and pry with all his strength before they could make an opening large enough to see what was inside.

"Looks like clothing," he said, dejected. "Just a heap of old clothes."

"Let's pull them out," Alison said.

"Why bother?" Eric felt depressed. His hopes had been so high. The last thing he wanted to find was a trunk of old clothes.

"We're searching, aren't we? Let's do a good job of it." She tugged at a piece of fabric, trying to pull it through the hole in the chest. "Pry another piece off and make the hole bigger, Eric."

With Terry's help, he tore away half the side. Then they pulled out the articles, one by one. The first was a brown hat with a wide brim. Then came a pair of long brown pants and a gray woolen jacket.

"They're all men's clothes," Alison said. "Wonder who they belonged to?" She held up a shirt made of some heavy, coarse material, "They even smell old."

Eric pulled out a heavy boot and set it on the ground.

"What are you doing, Alison?" Terry asked.

Eric looked up. She was unfolding another jacket and reaching into its pockets.

"Looking for papers," she said matter-of-factly. "So far I've found a handkerchief and a snuff box."

Eric shook his head. "The pirate's papers wouldn't be in . . ." He broke off, staring at her.

She had dropped the jacket, and in her hand was a folded scrap of paper. Carefully, she pulled it straight.

But it couldn't be what they were searching for, Eric thought as he watched her. Or could it?

9 • Scarab's Directions

Eric and Terry crowded around Alison, Eric shining the flashlight on the paper she held in her hands as she unfolded it with shaking fingers.

Eric's own fingers itched to do it himself. "Hurry up!"

"It's old and brittle. I don't want to tear it. Here, I've almost got it." She peeled off the last fold and held it out in front of her.

They all peered at it.

"That's it!" Terry shouted. "That's the one!"

And as the echoes of his cry bounced around the cave walls. Eric knew he was right. There was the same faint, brownish writing he'd seen before, and the jagged edge where the paper had been torn in half.

"The directions!" Eric cried. "Scarab's directions! What does it say?" In his excitement, Eric's hand darted out to take the paper, but she pulled it out of his reach.

"Be careful! You'll tear it! Let's get out of here so we can take a good look at it."

For a moment Eric felt anger. Did she want to keep those directions for herself? But the thought passed in his eagerness to read those long lost words and know at last where the treasure could be found. He hurried forward to light their way out of the cave.

"I knew we'd find it! I just knew it!" Alison said happily.

"Sure glad you didn't let those bats scare you off," Terry said. "Wait till the others hear about this!"

They were at the mouth of the cave now, Alison beside Eric, carrying the paper in her hand. As they came out, a breeze caught at it. The sheet fluttered.

"Be careful! You want it to blow into the water?" Eric reached for it. "Let me have it."

"It's OK." She gave him a puzzled look. "I'll take care of it." She folded it and tucked into the pocket of her blouse. "Safe and sound. Let's get back to the house so we can read it."

Terry turned away and loosened the bowline that moored the boat. "Get in and hold her at the dock for me, will you, Eric?"

Everything seemed to take so long, Eric thought, as he got into the boat and helped Alison in. Terry seemed to be moving in slow motion as he tossed him the bowline, then got into the boat himself. The paddles dipping into the water seemed slow and heavy. When they finally reached the rock ledge, Eric jumped out first. He was just about to start up the ladder when Terry called to him.

"Hey, can you find something to tie the boat to? I don't want it to wash out to sea."

"Oh, sure." He forced himself to look carefully around. "How about this?" Just under the ledge, a stalactite had formed. It looked solid enough.

"Fine. Here, catch." Terry threw him the bowline and Eric fastened it.

Now they could climb that ladder and go back along the passage to the house. Eric led the way.

"Wonder what we'll find in that treasure chest?" Terry said behind him. "Gold and jewels?"

"Dad told us about a gold cross with rubies," Alison said.

"I think there was money, too. Eric, did they use gold for money back in those days?"

"I guess so." Once again, the picture of a chest overflowing with riches hovered in the back of his mind. As soon as they could put the two halves of that paper together, in just a few minutes, the treasure would be as good as his.

"Wonder what the others will say when they hear?" Terry said.

The others. They'd have to tell Aunt Barbara and Nell and James and Dan and everyone else in their families. They'd all have to see the two halves of the directions put together. They'd all want to have part of the treasure, too. If only he could keep their find a secret, Eric thought.

"Keep the light still, Eric," Alison told him. "You're flashing it all over the place. It's hard to see the steps."

Her voice scattered his thoughts and he felt ashamed. Why did he keep thinking of that treasure as being his? How could he tell about the thoughts of the chest overflowing with gold and jewels that keep crowding into his brain? He wanted to hold them in his hands, to feel them and know they belonged to him.

What was the matter with him? Did Terry and Alison have the same thoughts?

Suddenly his light went out. Exclamations came from behind him as Terry and Alison stopped. He shook the flashlight, then discovered that when he pressed the switch, it turned on again. He'd been holding it so tightly, he'd flicked it off without meaning to!

"Sorry," he said.

"We should have brought extra flashlights," Terry said.

"Hey, when you're looking for treasure maps, it's hard to remember anything else," Alison said. "Eric, let's not forget to put this light back in the boat. Dan and Nell will need it."

How could they chatter so casually this way? Eric could

feel his heart pounding as they made their way up the steps. Soon they'd know where to find the treasure! Didn't they feel as excited as he did? "Let's go on up to the collection room," he told them. "Then we can go up to my tower and get the two halves together right now."

"OK," Terry agreed. "Then we can show the whole thing to the others."

The climb became steeper as they neared the second floor, but Eric hurried ahead. He easily found the lever that moved the suit of armor across the opening once more so that they could climb up through the small space. Then they raced through the collection room and made their way to the tower.

Alison sat on Eric's bed and took the folded paper from her pocket, smoothing it out on the bedspread. Terry sat beside her, while Eric opened the briefcase and pulled out the framed half of the directions he had there. He placed that on the bed. "Lay the other half over the glass, Alison, We can read the whole thing that way."

Alison carefully fitted the half sheet over the framed document, holding it in place with her fingers at the top and bottom while they all read it silently.

Lat. 37°   Long. 122°
There is a road leading from the walled
fort. Follow it southwest to where the
boulder rises from the hill in the shape
of a lion's head. Turn through a grove
of trees and you will find a church of
no great size but well attended on a
Sunday. Go on or near Midsummer's
day. Find the stained glass window shaped
like a rose with a blue heart. At sunset
the blue light will point out a stone in
the wall. Push against this and a stair
will be revealed. Look for the name that

means a star. Under this you will find
your entire fortunes with every piece there.
When you do, my soul will be freed of its
torment.

Eric finished reading it, and his hopes fell. The directions were so vague! They didn't tell where the lion's head boulder might be. They didn't name the fort or the church. "How can we find it from this?" he said aloud. "We're just about back where we started."

Alison nodded solemnly.

Terry looked disappointed, too. "A boulder in the shape of a lion's head," he murmured. "I've lived most of my life here and I've never seen anything like that. Or a church with that kind of window, either."

"Are we even sure the treasure's hidden around here?" Alison said. "Now that we have the longitude as well as the latitude, we'd better look them up. Do you have a map?"

"Aunt Barbara might have one. Come on, we'll ask her."

"Wait a minute." Eric unfastened the back of the leather frame and placed the two halves of the directions together inside it. "We won't lose it or tear it this way," he said, fastening the frame again.

A delicious smell came from the kitchen, and they glanced in as they passed. Aunt Barbara wasn't there. They went on to the living room and found her there, sewing the hem on a blue dress.

"Well, how is your search going?" she asked.

"We found the other half of the directions!" Terry announced.

"You did?" She looked astonished.

They described their search from the beginning, and she listened with great interest. When they told her about the bats, she looked worried. "I can see your scratches. Good thing the bats didn't bite you, though I haven't heard of a case of rabies around this area for years."

71

They told her the rest of their story. Then Eric handed her the frame that held the complete document.

She read it through silently, then looked up. "This church . . ."

"Do you know where it is?" Eric asked.

"No . . . that was so many years ago. The church might be gone now. Or a large church building might be built there in its place."

"Is there a map around?" Terry asked. "We want to look up these coordinates just to be sure it's even this area Scarab's talking about."

"There's got to be a map in my father's office. Terry, go find James, will you? I want him to see this, too. He's in his workshop. In the meantime, we'll get the map."

"Sure." Terry hurried out of the room, and Aunt Barbara wheeled her chair out the doorway and along the hall, with Eric and Alison behind her.

"How on earth did you think of looking in the pockets of those clothes, Alison? That was clever of you."

"I stuff pieces of paper in my pockets all the time." Alison looked pleased at the compliment. "I thought everyone else must do that, too."

"I wonder why an old trunk of clothes would be down there?" Aunt Barbara moved her chair to the bookcase beside the secret panel.

"We had a trunk of old clothes in the playroom, I remember. Maybe you saw it while you were up there. Used them for costumes, you know, and playing dress-up, and for Halloween. But none of those had anything in their pockets that I remember." She ran her finger along the bottom row of books, reading the titles. "I wonder if those clothes in the cave could have been John Roberts's things? Maybe when my great-grandfather built the house he just stored them away down there. Here. The World Atlas." She pulled out an oversized volume and set it on the desk. "Now let's look up the California coast and see what it says."

Eric and Alison studied the page with her. Latitude 37 went several miles north of Monterey and covered a large area. Longitude 122 intersected Santa Cruz, north of Monterey, and went on down near Pacific Grove and Carmel before extending south through the ocean.

"Well," Alison sighed, "at least we know for sure it's in this neighborhood, but Scarab didn't make the coordinates any more exact than his directions."

"Unless Nell remembers where Lion's Head Rock is, we're going to have to search for miles," Eric said.

Aunt Barbara replaced the book, and Eric pushed her wheelchair as they left the office.

"Nell told us Dan knows of a church where some pirate is buried," Alison said as they went along the hall. "Do you think that could be the same church?"

"We're not even sure it's the same pirate," Eric said.

Aunt Barbara looked up at him. "There must be hundreds of churches in this area. No, it seems to me your best clue is the rock. I'm sure Nell will remember where it is."

"I sure hope so." Eric pushed the wheelchair into the living room, then went to one of the huge windows to look out at the restless ocean. He felt just as restless. If Nell didn't remember, they'd have to start hiking up and down the coast.

Terry came back with James, and they showed him the paper and told him how they'd found it. He too seemed baffled by the directions.

"I know of a Lion's Head Inn," he said, "but it's close to San Francisco."

"Is there a Lion's Head Rock there, too?" Terry asked hopefully.

"Nope."

"That's too far north, anyway," Eric said. "We looked up the coordinates in the atlas. They're right along this coast between Santa Cruz and Big Sur."

"That's a long way!" Terry said.

"Yeah, but if the fort Scarab referred to is in Monterey, that cuts down on the distance. The rock and the church are somewhere south of it."

"Why don't we phone Dan and Nell right now," Aunt Barbara suggested. She wheeled her chair to the phone, on a small table near the door.

Alison came to stand beside Eric. "Tomorrow, I guess we should go to that fort. Was it Fort Mervine?"

"Yeah, unless you have any better ideas. It's strange that nobody seems to recognize anything—the church, or the rock."

"A hundred years is a long time."

Aunt Barbara was talking. "They found it, Nell! Isn't that wonderful? Yes, the other half of the pirate's directions to the treasure. Well, I'll let them tell you about it." She listened, then smiled. "Oh? Really? I know they'll be thrilled. Just a minute." She took the phone from her ear and beamed at all of them. "Nell says she's remembered something about Lion's Head Rock."

10 • The Pirate's Grave

Eric hurried for the phone, with Alison a close second, but Terry beat them to it. He grabbed the receiver and spoke excitedly into it. "You remember, Aunt Nell? About Lion's Head Rock?"

There was an intense silence while Terry listened, Eric held his breath, and Alison fidgeted with a strand of her hair. Even James and Aunt Barbara looked eager.

Terry was nodding. "Oh. I see." A long pause. "OK, wait a minute till I write it down." He opened the drawer and pulled out a pad and pencil. "OK. How do you spell it? . . . Yeah, we found the other half of the directions. Here, I'll read you the whole thing." He turned to Alison. "Can you give me those directions? Uncle Dan's on the extension, too. They both want to hear them."

"Sure." Alison got the framed document from the table and handed it to him.

Terry read it while Eric wished he'd end the conversation and tell them about the rock, but it was a few minutes longer before he hung up the phone.

"Well?" Eric said. "What did she say? Does she know where the rock is?"

"She knows where it *was*." Terry sat down on the couch next to James. "It isn't there any more."

"Then what were you writing?" Alison asked.

Terry held out the paper he was holding. Alison took it and Eric looked over her shoulder. There were four words written on it: *Christ Church. Hippolyte Richard.*

"That's the name of the church and the pirate who's buried there," Terry went on. "Uncle Dan looked them up for us. As soon as Aunt Nell saw the name of the church, she remembered about an earthquake that happened around twenty years ago. It shook up the town a bit, but the church and Lion's Head Rock got hit the hardest. The rock fell over the cliff into the ocean, and the church was wrecked."

"The Lion's Head Rock was near this church? And the pirate's buried there?" Eric's hopes soared. "Christ Church has to be the place where the treasure's hidden! How badly was it wrecked? Is it still there?"

"Uncle Dan said the graveyard's still there. He didn't say what else."

"Do you know where it is?" Alison asked him.

He nodded. "They told me how to get to it. It isn't far from here."

"Then let's go!" Eric said anxiously.

"Just a minute, kids," Aunt Barbara said. "Dinner will be ready soon. Why don't you wait and go tomorrow?"

"I'm not really hungry," Eric said. He looked at Alison and Terry, who agreed.

"It'll be light for a couple more hours," Terry said. "We can get there and back before dark."

She looked doubtful. "But how are you going to get there?"

Terry turned to James. "Would you lend us one of your cars, James? If we promise to take good care of it?"

He looked at Terry a long moment before he slowly nodded. "OK. But take it easy."

"You know I'm a good driver." Terry said. "I promise."

"Those are valuable cars," Aunt Barbara said. "I don't know that you should, James."

"He's a good driver. He should be. I taught him."

She sighed, then smiled. "Well I suppose my pot roast will keep until you get back."

Terry went to his aunt and kissed her cheek affectionately. "Honest, we'll be careful."

"Aren't you going to show me those names Dan gave you?"

"Oh, sure." He handed her the paper.

"Hippolyte Richard," she read. "That's the pirate's name?"

"Shouldn't it be Richard Hippo—whatever?" Alison wrinkled her nose.

Terry shook his head. "Uncle Dan spelled it for me and said that was it."

"That has to be Scarab's real name, then," Eric mused, "if Christ Church is where the treasure's hidden."

"No wonder they called him Scarab," Alison said.

"If the old church was wrecked by the earthquake," Aunt Barbara said, "I doubt you'll find the treasure there now. We have to be realistic, don't we?"

Why did "realistic" always mean *pessimistic,* Eric wondered, but he knew she could be right.

After they'd washed their scratched hands and faces quickly and applied the antiseptic Aunt Barbara gave them, they raced to James' workshop to borrow his car. He lent them the old De Soto and in a few minutes Terry was driving it slowly down the road. Alison had Scarab's directions tucked into her shoulder bag, although they all knew them by heart now.

"How far is it?" Eric looked at the sun, which was already low on the horizon.

"Four or five miles," Terry said. "We'll be there in ten minutes."

"If enough of the church is still standing so that rose window is there, we've got it made," Alison said. "It's close to Midsummer's Day—only two more weeks."

"And we'll be there at sunset, so we can see where the light goes through the blue heart of the window!" Eric was getting more excited. That window had to be there! Then they could get the treasure tonight! "Can't you drive faster?" he asked Terry. "There's hardly any traffic."

"James said I couldn't take it over forty miles an hour, and if anything happened to his car, he'd never speak to me again."

Eric tried to relax against the seat, but he was so tense, so excited, he felt he wanted to get out and push the car.

"Maybe only part of the church was wrecked," Alison said. "Maybe only the steeple fell off, or something."

"But the treasure has to be there anyway," Eric told her. "The directions said we'd find stairs that led to it. If they go down, the treasure's hidden under the church."

"The stairs would have to go down," Alison said. "Upstairs would only be the choir loft or the bell tower, wouldn't it?"

Terry turned off the highway onto a dirt road. It was deserted and nearly overgrown with weeds, and it meandered across the low hills toward the ocean. When they came to a grove of cypress and pine, Eric craned his neck to see what lay beyond.

"That must be the grove Scarab mentioned," he said. "Where's the church?"

They had come out into a little green valley. To the west, the rocks rose, sheltering it from the sea, and in front of them was a stone wall with an iron gate. They stopped the car, jumped out, and found to their relief the gate wasn't locked. They pushed it open.

Gravestones stretched row on row across the grass, shaded by trees and flowering bushes. Footpaths wandered between them, and in the distance Eric could see a building surrounded by trees. He pointed to it. "Could that be the church?"

"It looks too small," Alison said, doubtfully.

"Maybe it just looks small from here," Terry said. "Let's go!"

They ran along the path toward it, but it wasn't the church. It was no more than a small cottage with a shingle roof. There was no other structure in sight.

"The church isn't even here!" Alison said. "Are you sure this is the right place, Terry?"

"Sure I'm sure. Uncle Dan told me to turn off the main road at Herron's Lane and keep on until we came to the gate. This is a short cut. There's another way into the cemetery from the highway. The main parking lot's over there."

"And he said this is where Christ Church is supposed to be?" Eric asked him.

"That's what he said. Anyway, the cemetery is here."

Eric thought for a moment. "OK, then. The best thing we can do is go up on that slope over there and see what we can see."

In five minutes they had reached the top of the rocky cliff over the ocean, and could look down on the valley, illuminated by the long rays of the setting sun. But Eric could see no sign of a church.

"The church was wrecked, all right." Alison's voice was low and sad. "Wrecked right down to the ground."

"I can see part of the foundation," Terry said. "I think that's what it is, anyway."

Eric looked where Terry was pointing. Near the small building he could see a dark ridge running straight across the grass. Now he could even make out another ridge, at right angles to the first. "But the building's gone," he said. "The window, the stairs—all gone."

They stood silently as the waves crashed on the rocks below and the cool sea breeze sighed through the dead tree's branches.

"Come on," Eric said. "Let's go."

"But if those stairs did go down," Alison said as they walked, more slowly now, down the slope, "then you might be right. The treasure might still be here."

"So how do we find it?" Eric asked her. "We can't dig up everything, can we? And what about the name that means a star? It's all buried somewhere under there, but we might never find it."

They went to the place where the ridge had shown in the grass, nearing the small building.

"Yep, it's the church's foundation." Eric pushed at the ridge with the toe of his sneaker. "That shack is built right over where the church used to be."

Alison peered through the window. "Could it be a caretaker's house?"

Eric and Terry went to look over her shoulder.

"It isn't a house," Eric said. "It's too small. I think he just keeps his tools and equipment in here."

"But there's a cot and a desk with a radio," Alison said.

"He likes to take naps," Terry suggested.

"Well, as long as we're here, I want to see the pirate's grave." Alison started along the closest path. "Maybe there's some clue on his gravestone."

Eric stayed where he was. "That's a last resort if I ever heard one!" Discouragement was taking hold. His body felt slow and heavy. He wanted to crawl into a hole and stay there. No church, no window, and no chance of ever finding the treasure now. It was all too much.

But Terry was following Alison. "That's an idea. We could at least take a look."

"Do you know where the grave is?" she asked him.

"No. Just that it's here somewhere."

Their voices faded as they went along the path. Eric stayed by the little building, his thoughts dark. Let them search. It was useless. Probably the caretaker would be the only one who would know where any particular grave might be. Maybe even he wouldn't know. The pirate's grave had been here for a hundred years. He leaned against the wooden wall of the cottage and wondered if the caretaker had been here when the earthquake happened. This shack of his couldn't have been here then, since it was built right on the site of the church. . . . He straightened suddenly. But if the caretaker had been here twenty years ago, when it happened, he might know a few things about the church, too.

"Hey!" he shouted to the others. "Wait!"

He ran along the path, seeing Alison's yellow blouse clearly in the deepening twilight.

"What's the matter?" she asked as he came closer. "See a ghost or something?"

"I see the ghost of a *chance*. A slim one, maybe, but still a chance." He took a couple of deep breaths, then went on. "The caretaker of this place might know where the stairs were behind the stone. Especially if he was working here when the earthquake happened."

Terry and Alison watched him silently.

"Well," he went on, "do you see what I mean? If the church collapsed and they cleared away the debris, he would have seen the stairway going down, wouldn't he?"

Alison rubbed her ear, thoughtfully. "Maybe. If the stairs did go down. But the earthquake could have destroyed them completely, too, Eric."

"It doesn't look like it disturbed the graveyard."

Terry grinned. "So if the caretaker knows where the stairs are, maybe we can get to them. Maybe the place they lead to is still there, under the ground." Then his grin faded. "But we'd still have to do a lot of digging to get into it, wouldn't we?"

Eric shrugged. "I don't know. Let's worry about one thing at a time. Let's just find out if he knows anything, then we can go from there."

"Right!" Alison agreed. "We can come back here

tomorrow and talk to the caretaker, and see what we can find out."

"If we don't find the pirate's grave before it's too dark," Terry said, "we can ask the caretaker about that, too."

"It should be in this part of the cemetery," she said, studying another marker. "These all seem to date back to the 1800's."

Eric watched them, puzzled. "I still don't see why you want to find it, Alison."

"Just to prove that it really is Scarab. Then I'd be sure this is the right place."

Eric followed them, but although they covered several rows of gravestones, the name Hippolyte Richard was not there. Finally it got so dark they could barely make out the inscriptions.

"We'd better leave now," he said, "while we can still see the way out."

They walked back along the path toward the gate through the silent cemetery, the sea breeze rustling the leaves around them, the sky deep blue now and sprinkled with stars. Alison stopped to tie one of her shoelaces, and Terry waited beside her. Eric walked slowly on. He glanced toward the caretaker's cottage just ahead, blinked, and looked again.

Somebody was standing beside it—someone who wore a white shirt that glowed in the darkness. The caretaker? He hurried toward it. As he came closer he could see that the person whoever it was, had his back turned. He wore a strange-looking hat with a long feather, and he was looking through the window of the little building.

"Hey!" Alison called to Eric. "Wait a minute. What's the rush?"

The figure turned abruptly. Eric was close enough to see it plainly now. He stopped and stared.

Not only the white shirt, but the whole body shimmered with an unearthly luminescence. Eric could see the ruffles on the shirt, the knee-breeches held by a jeweled belt and the sword that was buckled there. The figure moved his hand, and a huge jewel on his forefinger sparkled.

Eric was barely conscious that Alison and Terry had come up beside him and were watching the figure, too. Fear froze him so that he couldn't move. He could only stare, as the ghost of the pirate moved toward them.

11 • The Ghost

Eric, horrified, watched the ghost of the pirate move slowly toward them through the trees. Alison, beside him, gripped his arm with fingers of ice. On his other side, Terry made a terrified sound deep in his throat.

The ghost seemed to float in that unearthly, shimmering glow. His bearded face was half-hidden by the hat's broad brim, but Eric thought he could see a mocking smile there.

"Scarab!" The name forced itself past the lump in his throat. "Scarab!"

The figure stopped, threw back his head, and a flood of mocking laughter resounded through the night.

Suddenly Eric was running, pounding down the path, away from that fearful sight, towing Alison along with him by the hand, Terry racing beside them. They streaked across the cemetery, not waiting to find the paths, not stopping to catch their breath, until at last the gate was just ahead of them. Once through it, Eric yanked open the car door and the three of them leaped inside in a tangle of arms and legs.

While Terry fumbled in his pockets for the ignition key,

Eric pressed his nose to the windshield and searched the darkness for sight of the pirate's ghost.

"Did he follow us?" Alison panted.

"No. I don't know. I don't see him." Eric rubbed away the mist his breath had left and peered through the smeared circle. "Hurry up, Terry!"

"I am! I can't find the key!"

"Lock the doors!" Alison cried.

"Here it is!" Terry made scraping sounds as he tried to fit the key into the lock. "It won't go. I can't . . . oh, OK." The key slid into position. He turned it. The motor made grinding noises, stopped, then ground again.

"Gas!" Alison whispered urgently. "Give it gas!"

Terry pumped furiously on the accelerator and the motor came to life. The car jerked suddenly backward, coughed, and died.

Alison moaned.

Terry got the motor started once more and turned on the headlights. The beams cut through the darkness. There was only a wall and a gate, with the trees and the gravestones beyond. He let out his breath and swerved the car around.

Once they were heading back toward the main road, Eric pushed his damp hair off his forehead and found he could breathe normally again. "You saw it, didn't you? Scarab's ghost!"

"I didn't know there could be such a thing," Alison said. "I . . . I never believed in ghosts."

"Me neither," Terry said.

Eric could suddenly feel every part of his body tingling with relief. "I was sure he was following us."

"Me too." The steering wheel moved out of Terry's hands and the car wobbled before he grabbed the wheel again.

"Be careful!" Alison said sharply.

"Sorry. My hands don't seem to be working right. I'm still sort of shaky."

After a while, she said, "No one's going to believe us when we tell them we saw a ghost."

"What else could it have been?" demanded Terry. "We all saw it."

"Well, we've been through a lot today. Maybe it was something we ate."

"We didn't eat," Terry pointed out. "Except breakfast."

"Then something we didn't eat. Hallucinations. Starving people have hallucinations, don't they?"

Eric stared at the lights on the main road just ahead. "Maybe, but we couldn't all have the same hallucination."

They turned onto the highway.

"If he's a ghost, then is he haunting the place where the treasure's buried," Eric said, "or haunting us?"

"Could be he's warning us not to try to find the treasure," Terry said.

"He wouldn't do that. He wants us to *find* it, remember?"

"Then you think he might have been trying to tell us where it is?" Terry asked.

"All he did was laugh. That doesn't tell us much."

"Well," Alison said firmly, "I think he's just some kind of electronic machine the cemetery people have set up to keep out night visitors."

Eric hadn't even thought of that. Alison had a more skeptical nature than he did. But he couldn't believe that ghost had been a machine. Not the way it had looked at him, and the way it had laughed.

When they reached the house and drove the De Soto back to the garage, they looked into the workshop. It was dark. James must have stopped work for the night. They went on into the house. There was a light outside the front door for them and the hall light was on, but the rest of the house was in darkness.

"Wonder where they are?" Eric followed the other two as they went to the kitchen.

"Maybe they went to see a movie." Terry switched on the kitchen light. There was a note on the table, propped against a bunch of carnations in a vase.

> I had one of my headaches, so have gone to bed.
> Your dinner is in the oven. Thanks so much, Eric
> and Alison, for the lovely flowers.
> Love,
> Aunt Barbara

Terry glanced at his watch. "It's after nine. James is probably out somewhere with friends." He looked disappointed. "I thought they'd be waiting to hear about what we found."

Alison yawned. "Well, I wouldn't mind going to bed a bit early myself." She opened the oven and looked at the pot roast and vegetables keeping warm in a casserole dish. "Mmmm. Dinner and bed. Best things in the world."

They each heaped a plate with food and sat down at the kitchen table. "Maybe we should call Dan and Nell," Eric said. "They're probably waiting to hear from us."

Terry stuffed a large chunk of potato into his mouth, then got up to go to the phone on the wall. He dialed, listened for a moment, then hung up. "No answer there. They must be out."

"I get the feeling nobody's really as anxious about this treasure hunt as we are," Alison said.

"Could be they don't really believe we'll find it." Eric buttered a piece of bread. "Maybe they're right. How do you guys feel about going back to the cemetery?" He looked from Alison to Terry.

"I don't mind, if it's daylight." Alison said "How do you feel, Terry?"

"I think we ought to go back and talk to the caretaker, the way we planned." He stifled a yawn. "But right now, I want to go to bed."

In spite of the excitement of the day, Eric fell quickly into a sound sleep in his tower room. When he awoke in the morning, the windows were blank with fog. They couldn't do much in weather like this, he thought as he washed and dressed. Still he felt cheerful. The fog would have to lift some time.

Aunt Barbara said she was feeling much better, and over breakfast they told her and James about the ruined church.

She shook her head sadly. "Doesn't seem like there's much chance of finding those heirlooms now. That's a real shame. Is there nothing left of the church at all?"

"Only the foundation." Terry paused, then went on with a glance at James. "You probably won't believe this, but we saw a ghost in the cemetery last night."

Eric, too, had been sure James would laugh. He was surprised at his matter-of-fact acceptance. "What did it look like?" was all he said.

"It looked like a pirate," Alison told him. "But I don't think it was really a ghost."

Aunt Barbara raised her eyebrows. "What do you think it was, Alison?"

"Probably some electronic figure to keep out trespassers. You know, the kind they have in Disneyland and some other places? Dummies that talk and move."

"In a graveyard?" Aunt Barbara registered disbelief. "Why would they go to all that expense? There's nothing to steal in a graveyard."

"Well, they have a caretaker there. I guess he doesn't want anyone breaking into his cottage and stealing his stuff."

"It had this strange sort of glow," Eric said. "I don't think anyone would rig up an electronic figure to look like a ghost, Alison. It would scare people to death. Anyway, if they want to keep out trespassers, they could just keep the gates locked."

"It looked like a real ghost to me," Terry said.

"Well, it could have been a ghost," Aunt Barbara said. "There are strange things in this world."

Eric nodded. "Anyway, we want to go back today and talk to the caretaker. He might know a way we can get at the treasure." He glanced at the fog pressing thickly against the windows. "That is, we *were* going, but this fog . . ."

"It'll burn off by ten or eleven." James got up from the table. "You can borrow the De Soto again if you need it."

"Oh, Terry, you should call Dan and Nell and tell them about all this," Aunt Barbara said. "Dan was on the phone first thing this morning wanting to know if you'd found anything."

After breakfast, Terry phoned them and told them the whole story. "They weren't very surprised about the church," he told Eric and Alison when he was through. "And I don't think they really believed that we saw the ghost. Uncle Dan said we must be all keyed up, what with all we've been through. Oh, and he said don't worry about getting their boat back today since they won't need it for a while."

The fog didn't dissipate until mid-afternoon, but as soon as they could, they borrowed the De Soto and set out for the cemetery.

"I've been thinking," Alison told them as they drove along the road. "If we ask this caretaker questions, we'll have to tell him about the treasure, won't we?"

"We can't do that!" Terry seemed alarmed. "He might just say he doesn't know anything about it, and then use our directions to find it himself."

"I had the same thought," Eric said. "The only thing I can think of to do is tell him we're interested in the history of old Monterey and the pirate who lived here."

"I could tell him I'm going to write a story about the pirate," Terry said. "That's the truth." ·

"That's good," Eric agreed. "But he'd want to know how we know about the stairway. . . . How about telling him you going to write about the church and the pirate who's buried there? That way we can ask all sorts of questions."

"Great!" Terry grinned. "Since the church is where the treasure's buried, that's the truth, too."

When they arrived at the cemetery, the sun was warm and the sky clear. The door to the caretaker's cottage was still closed, but they could hear the motor of the lawn mower not far away. They followed the sound and in a few minutes they saw him.

He sat on the seat of the large machine, a slim, gray-haired man wearing a blue shirt under his overalls. When they came closer, they waved and called to him. He stopped the motor, got down from his seat, and came toward them.

"Yes?" His voice was thin and wavering. "What can I do for you?"

He looked very old and frail, Eric noticed. He could certainly have been here for twenty years, or even longer.

"We're looking for the grave of a pirate who's supposed to be buried here." Terry said. He pulled the piece of paper from his pocket with the pirate's name on it and showed it to the man.

He raised his white eyebrows in surprise. "Hippolyte Richard? Why do you want to see his grave? Who are you?"

"My name's Terry Roberts. This is Alison Thorne and her brother Eric."

"Eric Thorne?" The caretaker wheezed and began to cough. It was a few moments before he was able to stop. Then he stared at Eric, looking him up and down.

Eric felt uncomfortable, and wondered why this man was looking at him so strangely. Why had he seemed surprised when they asked about the pirate's grave? He shook the caretaker's hand, and it felt limp and bony. "Everyone calls me Al," the man said.

"We're interested in seeing the grave," Terry said, "because I'm doing research for a story about Christ Church and a pirate whose nickname was Scarab. Do you know if it's the same man?"

"The grave's right over here. Look for yourselves." He led them to a grave under a tree. The gravestone was rough and dark, the words on it blurred with age.

Here Lies
Hippolyte J. Richard
Born September 10, 1823
Died March 29, 1887
May his Soul Rest in Peace

"Is that a beetle?" Alison asked, pointing to the mark next to the words.

"It's a scarab beetle," Eric said quietly. He was conscious that Al kept glancing at him.

"Not many people know he was called Scarab," Al said, speaking directly to Eric, "or even that he was once a pirate. He reformed, you know. Settled down and raised a family. Ran an honest business. Went to church regular. No, not many people know. How come you do?"

"We . . . uh . . . read about him," Eric stammered.

Al's stare was cold and penetrating. "I don't believe you," he said.

12 • The Hidden Staircase

The caretaker folded his arms and regarded Eric suspiciously. "How do you know that Hippolyte Richard was once a pirate called Scarab?" he repeated. "That name was kept secret after he came ashore to live an honest life."

Terry spoke up. "I ran across his name in some old papers when I was doing research for my book."

Al turned his icy stare on him. "What old papers?"

"Well . . . I saw a letter he signed."

"How did he sign it?" the old man asked indignantly.

"He just signed it 'Scarab,' but . . ." Terry broke off, glancing helplessly at Eric and Alison.

"That scarab symbol is right there on his gravestone," Eric finished for him. "Anyone could see that."

"You knew both his real name and his secret name before you ever saw his gravestone!" Al said angrily. He waited for an answer, and when Eric and the others couldn't give one, his wrinkled face showed his disapproval. "You are lying to me," he told them. "Trying to make a fool of an old man." With that, he turned and went back to his lawn mower.

When the motor started again, Eric beckoned the other two to follow him down the path to a place where they could talk without shouting. Then he stopped under a tree and shook his head slowly. "I feel about an inch high."

"But we weren't lying to him!" Terry's face had reddened under his tan.

"No," Alison agreed, "but we were trying to get information from him without giving him any. It's almost the same thing."

"I think we should show him Scarab's directions," Eric said. "Tell him exactly what we're doing. Do you still have them in your purse, Alison?"

"They're right here." She patted her shoulder bag.

"But then, if he knows the way to those stairs, he could lie to *us* and keep the treasure himself!" Terry objected.

Eric rubbed his earlobe thoughtfully. "He could, but it looks like we'll have to take that chance. He's not going to tell us anything unless we tell him the whole truth, and without his help, we might never find the treasure."

"I don't think he'd try to take it for himself," Alison said.

"He's so crabby, he might do anything." Terry jammed his hands into his jeans pockets, scowling. "How did *he* know that Scarab was the pirate's secret name? He didn't tell us *that*, did he?"

"That's true, he didn't," Eric said. "Or why he should get so angry about a pirate who's been dead for so many years."

"Maybe there's another way to find those stairs," Terry said.

"Got any ideas?" Eric wished he had some himself.

Terry strode a few paces away from them and looked in the direction of the ruined church. He stayed there for a long moment, his shoulders hunched stubbornly. Then he turned back to them. "OK. Show him the directions. Only I don't trust him."

"We'll just tell him those are our family heirlooms and

they're legally ours." Alison opened her purse and pulled out the framed directions. "This even says so."

"Oh, great." Terry didn't sound convinced. "That's going to do a lot of good."

Eric laughed, feeling relieved. He wasn't anxious to share their secret with anyone, either, but Al seemed like their last hope of finding a way to get at the treasure. He probably wouldn't be able to help them at all, but who could tell?

They had a hard time trying to coax Al into talking to them again. He glanced coldly at them and steered his lawn mower around them as they waved and shouted. Finally Alison ran beside him and held up the framed document. He cut the motor with an unfriendly expression and spoke gruffly. "Well? What is it now?"

"Here," Alison said. "This is one of the old letters from Scarab that Terry told you about. We want to show it to you and tell you the whole story."

He looked around at all of them, his eyes still suspicious but his tone a little more friendly. "That so? Well, all right." He took the frame and squinted at it. "Can't read it without my glasses, though. You can come on down to my cabin. That's where I keep them."

They followed him as he slowly made his way toward the cottage, Terry still looking reluctant and Alison a little worried. Eric knew how they felt, but his hope was stronger than his fear. "Have you been caretaker here for a long time?" he asked.

"Pretty near twenty years, now."

"Then you must have been here during the earthquake?"

"That was a bit before my time," Al said, "but I remember when it happened, well enough. Right around five o'clock in the morning. Lucky nobody was in the church at that hour. The whole choir loft caved in and crashed down on top of the pews, organ and all." He shook his head at

94

the memory. "They had some time clearing away the wreckage, I can tell you. Awful shame, it was. The whole congregation turned out to help, and a lot of us were sad to see the old place go like that. There was plenty of talk about trying to rebuild the church right here, but they decided to salvage what they could and put up a new building in town."

They had reached the cottage, and he fished a key from his overalls pocket to unlock the door, fumbling with the handle, talking in his high, wavering voice as he let them in. "That's when the pastor asked me to come out here and care for the cemetery. Lucky most of the graves weren't disturbed. That was a couple of months after they'd retired me from my job at the fish cannery, so I was right glad to get the work."

They had to walk up two wooden steps just inside the door. While the caretaker carried the framed document to the desk next to the cabin's only window, Eric, Alison, and Terry stood on the top step and looked around.

As small as the place seemed from the outside, Eric could see it was partitioned off into four rooms. The main room, where they stood, held the cot and a chair besides the desk, and opened onto a tiny, square hall where three closed doors formed three sides of the square. One would probably be a bathroom, he thought. Would the other two be storage rooms?

"I spend three or four days a week looking after the cemetery," Al went on as he opened the desk drawer, found his glasses, and put them on. "Keeps me active. At my age, this is pretty good exercise. And I get to talk to the folks who come and visit the graves." He sat in the chair and picked up the pirate's directions. "Now, let's see what this is all about." With a look of concentration on his weather-beaten face, he read the words silently, while Terry shifted feet impatiently and Alison leaned against the wall. When he was through, he looked up at them.

"I remember that rose window with the blue center. Very old. It was made in France and set in the church about 1829. The quake shattered in into a million pieces."

"You see the signature on that paper?" Terry asked him. "Scarab. He took our families' treasures from them when he pirated the ship they were on."

"Where did you get this?" Al asked him.

"Scarab sent half to the Thorne family and half to the Robertses." Terry went to stand beside Al's chair and pointed to the place where the jagged edges of the document had been put together. "See? He tore it right down the middle."

"Scarab's been dead since 1887." Al looked suspiciously at them. "If he sent this letter, he didn't send it to you."

"No," Eric said, "he sent it to our ancestors—the people he robbed," and patiently he told the story, beginning with Terry's composition and ending with the finding of the half-document in the cavern.

The old caretaker listened, pushing his reading glasses down to the end of his nose so he could study Eric's face as he spoke, and nodding every now and then. When Eric had finished, he pursed his lips and tapped his forefinger on the desk, thoughtfully.

"So you came here looking for your families' goods, did you?" he said at last.

Eric nodded. "We came here yesterday evening and found the church had been ruined."

"And we saw Scarab's ghost here last night," Terry said.

"He was standing right here by your cottage. Just after dark," Eric glanced uneasily out the window at the sunlit trees where the ghost had stood.

"It wasn't really a ghost, though, was it?" Alison asked.

"I don't know what you might have seen." Al scratched his chin. "You say Scarab's ghost? Well, well." He seemed stunned at the news.

"You've never seen it?" Terry asked him.

"Nope. Never heard tell of a ghost around here, either."
Al removed his reading glasses and folded with with
shaking fingers. "You sure it was *Scarab?*"

"It was a pirate," Eric said. "He wore a hat with a
feather and a jeweled belt with a sword. We thought it
must be Scarab, since he's buried here. And that's how we
figured out that this Hippolyte Richard must be Scarab,
because of the treasure being hidden here, too."

"You don't have any kind of dummy rigged up to scare
people away?" Alison asked nervously.

"Nope. I just lock up this place about six o'clock.
Nobody's ever bothered anything."

"Well," Eric said, "anyway, we came back here today to
ask you if you know where those stairs are."

"Stairs?" The caretaker blinked at him.

"The ones that lead to the place the treasure is hidden."
Eric wished Terry had never mentioned the ghost.

Alison perched on the edge of the desk. "You know the
stairs Scarab mentions in those directions? We can't find
them by using the rose window now, so we thought that
since you know this place so well, you might know where
they are. If they're still intact, that is."

Al blinked again. "How do you know nobody came here
while the church was still standing and found this
treasure of yours?"

The words hit Eric like a blow. Disappointment made
him feel weak. "You mean somebody else took it?"

"I don't know," Al said. "I never heard anything about
any gold or jewels hidden in the church."

"But do you know about the stairs?" Eric asked breath-
lessly. "So we can go and see for ourselves?"

The caretaker rubbed his chin. "You come here telling
some mighty strange stories." His eyes darted suspiciously
from one to the other of them. "How do I know any of this
is the truth? How do I know you aren't making all this
up?"

"We didn't even want to tell you anything about it," Terry said angrily. "We just want to find what's rightfully ours. We had to break our necks to find these directions. How do we know, now that you've seen them, you won't just keep the whole treasure for yourself?"

"Anyway, we can verify all this," Eric said, more calmly. "Our families know about it too. If you like, we can get them to vouch for us."

Al nodded, smiling faintly. "All right, then. Tell you what. You give me some identification—a driver's license or something—and I might just believe you." He handed the framed paper back to Alison, leaned back, and folded his arms.

Hope rose in Eric again. "OK," he said. Maybe Al did know something, after all, the way he was smiling at them. He yanked his wallet out of his pocket and flipped through the cards inside it to find his driver's license, while Terry did the same and Alison searched her purse, putting the frame back inside it as she did so. Then each of them held out their identification for him to see.

He put his glasses on again and read their licenses, then removed the glasses, placed them carefully on his desk, and stood up. "All right," he said. "I guess I can show you the stairway."

13 • Star

"You *do* know where that stairway is?" Eric was stunned. He had hoped, but hadn't truly believed that the stairs could still be here, that the treasure might still be reclaimed. "Does it go down under the foundations? Is there anything left down there?"

"Where are they?" Terry cried at the same time. "Can we still use them?"

The caretaker paid them no attention. He shuffled to the little hallway, opened one of the doors, and switched on a light. Watching him, Eric could see that room was used for tool storage, just as he'd thought. Al pulled a large flashlight from a shelf, turned out the light, and came out again, closing the door carefully behind him. Then he made a quarter turn to face the next door, slid back a bolt that fastened it, and turned the handle. "Come on," he said as he opened the door. "Follow me. Watch your step."

Alison's eyes were shining. "How about *that!*"

"All right!" Terry followed her through the open door and Eric was close behind.

The stairway was dark and the wooden steps creaked ominously under their weight. Eric had to run his hand

99

along the dank stone wall and tread carefully, feeling for each step, since Al's light was far ahead of him. The smell of decaying earth and ancient stone surrounded them as they went downward.

"Where does this lead?" He heard Alison asking.

"To the crypt," Al answered. "Be careful. These walls are buckling in places."

At the bottom of the stairs he told them to wait, and they all stood in darkness while he took his flashlight a few paces away. There was the sound of a match striking, then a brighter light shone and he held up a kerosene lantern. "All right now," he said. "This is the crypt."

It was dark and airless, with a vaulted stone ceiling supported by marble pillars. Rectangular marble coffins stood in rows on the earthen floor.

"This was used for buryings when the church was first built," Al told them, "but after it got filled up they just never used it any more. It was long before my time."

"But how did you know about this, and those stairs?" Eric asked him. "Scarab wrote that this could only be found by moving a stone in the wall."

He nodded. "A few years after it was filled, they walled it up so nobody would come down here, but the earthquake broke down that wall, too. When they found the stairs, while they were clearing away the wreckage, they decided to build my cabin right over them so nobody else could find them. Out of respect for the dead, you know. Asked me to watch out for the crypt, here."

He moved his light from side to side so they could get a better view. "I don't come down here often. There's not much to do down here, of course. Not like out there. But I keep it up."

As he talked, Eric, Alison and Terry went to the nearest sarcophagus. It was about three feet high and six feet long, of white marble with an angel perching on the corner, the names of the deceased and the dates engraved on its top.

"These are really old," Terry said. "Look at these dates. 'Roger Miles, born June 21, 1781, died October 9, 1843.'"

"We have to find a name that means a star," Alison reminded them.

"Star," Al said and paused. "There's a Starling over there, I remember." He pointed to the darkness outside their circle of light. "Emma Starling."

Eric shook his head. "That wouldn't be it. I wonder if Scarab was talking about the name of a star. He was a sailor, so he probably knew a lot of the names for stars." Eric moved along the row of coffins, looking at the names. "But I never heard of anyone named *Sirius* or *Arcturus*."

"Maybe the name is another word for star," Alison suggested, reading another epitaph. "This one's Miguel Gomez. Can't be the right one."

"What's another word for star?" Terry asked. "Is there one?"

"I guess maybe 'planet' or 'asteroid,'" Alison said doubtfully.

"I never heard of anyone named 'Planet,' either," Terry said, moving ahead of him.

Eric paused to read another inscription. "Here's Lily and Samuel MacGregor."

"This one's Ada Orange," Alison said. "We don't have to guess about that one."

They moved along the row with Al following, holding the lantern high so they could read the faint engravings on the stones.

"Here's another Spanish name," Terry said. "Now I wish I'd taken Spanish in school. Tiburcio and Carmella Preciar." He stumbled over the unfamiliar words. "You guys know any Spanish?"

"Not much," Alison moaned. "We picked up a little of several different languages when we lived in Europe as kids, but I can't remember the word for 'star' in any of them. Can you, Eric?"

He, too, was wishing he'd paid more attention to learning the various languages they'd been exposed to. Right now, his impatience to find the treasure that was so close to them seemed to have driven everything else out of his mind. "We're just going to have to read every name and hope for the best," he said.

"I know a few words of Spanish," Al said.

Eric looked hopefully at him. "Do you remember the word for star?"

"Nope. Learned it mostly from the men I worked with at the canning factory. Don't think we ever did talk about the stars."

"Ludwig and Ludmilla Kiefer," Alison read. "Sounds German, but it doesn't sound like star, does it?"

"I don't think so," Eric said.

She touched his arm. "We could find it, Eric, and never know we did!"

She looked dejected, and though Eric was beginning to feel the same way, he tried to sound cheerful. "It's so close now, we're going to trip over it. Don't worry. We'll know."

"Here's Maria Ibarra," Terry said. "That can't be it."

Al coughed. "It gets cold down here," he said. "Cold and damp. Gets to my arthritis. Then I have a hard time climbing those stairs."

"We're doing this as fast as we can." Alison turned a sympathetic look toward him. "Would you like to wait upstairs for us?"

He considered a moment, then shook his head. "I guess I'll just stay with you. I'm responsible for what goes on here, you know. Only we can't stay much longer."

The hollow feeling in the pit of Eric's stomach grew more intense. Not only were they faced with all these foreign names, but now they had a time limit! "OK," he said. "If I can use your flashlight, Al, I'll go to another row. If we each take a different row and read the last names out loud maybe something will ring a bell."

"Flashlight's over there, by the stairs," Al pointed into the darkness.

Eric groped along the bottom step, found it, and shone the beam along the nearest wall. Here were nameplates, too, he hadn't noticed before. "Oh, no! Do we have to read all these, too?" They were small metal plates in vertical rows. "What are these, Al?"

"Coffins. Stacked eight or ten high and sealed into the wall."

"Osti," Alison sang out.

"Vallejo," Terry shouted.

Eric made a quick decision. There wouldn't be time, he was sure, to read all of these names on the wall, but the most likely place for Scarab to hide that treasure would be in one of the large stone caskets. He began the row closest to the wall.

"Gallagher," Alison called.

"Bramley," Terry announced. "I'm skipping the ones like Smith and Jones."

Eric went down his row, skimming the names that were familiar, pausing to consider each one that was strange. Like the name on the stone in front of him. It was engraved in shaky, uneven letters, unlike the firmly printed names on the other coffins, as thought scratched there by an unpracticed hand. *Stella Maris*. Something inside him throbbed. "Stella Maris," he repeated slowly. His mind speedily connected words and thoughts. He gave a sudden shout. "Hey, come here! I think I've found it!"

They crowded around him, Al holding up his lantern so they could all see the name clearly.

"Stella Maris?" Terry said. "Does that mean star?"

"Stella does." Eric's voice was shaky with excitement now. "Think about it. A constellation is a group of stars, right?"

Alison snapped her fingers. "Sure! And an actor has a stellar role when he stars in something."

"Interstellar travel!" Terry's face lit with excitement.

"Estrella!" Al said in a surprised voice. "That's star in Spanish!" He laughed. "I just remembered. We must have talked about stars after all."

Alison laughed with delight. Eric waved the flashlight in the air and shouted. "It's here! It's here!"

He was suddenly conscious that Al was saying something but none of them were paying attention. He turned to see that the old man was slowly shaking his head.

"You found a name that means 'star,'" Al said gravely, "but you haven't found any treasure that I can see."

They all stared at him.

Eric wasn't sure just what he meant. "It's right here, Al. Right in this coffin."

Al shook his head again. "Every one of these coffins is in my care. I can't let you go breaking into this one. What if there's a body inside? A body named Stella Maris?"

14 • In the Crypt

"No," Al said firmly. "I can't let you open this sarcophagus."

Eric was shocked. "But Scarab's hidden our heirlooms in
there! You saw his directions!"

"Yeah!" Terry looked stunned. "He stole the stuff from
our families."

"Sorry." The old caretaker shook his head. "This crypt is
church property. I'm responsible for everything here."

"But what's inside this tomb is our property." Alison
looked bewildered.

"You don't know for sure your heirlooms are inside
there."

"We have to find out!" She lifted her chin stubbornly.
"We've come here all the way from Illinois, and we've been
searching everywhere! This stuff has been missing for
more than a hundred years, and everyone in both our
families has wondered where it was. How can you say we
can't open this coffin and find out if it's in there?"

Al's face softened slightly as she talked, so that for a
moment Eric thought he might change his mind. He added
his argument to Alison's.

"You knew we were searching for the treasure. We told you that, and you said you'd help us."

Al turned abruptly away, taking his lantern with him. "I said I'd show you the stairs, and I did. Now come along."

"Crabby old man!" Terry muttered furiously as the caretaker walked away from them.

Alison seemed about to cry. "It's not fair!"

"I'd like to just stay here and open this coffin anyway," Terry said.

"Yeah. So would I, but we have to do as he says. He's in charge here." Eric shone the beam of the flashlight to guide their way. "We'll just have to try to think of something."

Al was moving slowly, halfway up the stairs. They followed him reluctantly. At the top he turned off the kerosene lantern and placed it on a shelf in the toolroom, then took the flashlight from Eric and placed that beside it. After he'd closed the toolroom door, he carefully drew the bolt across the door to the crypt while the others went into the main room of the cottage, blinking in the sudden sunlight.

Al hobbled in and eased himself into the chair in front of the desk. "Time for me to quit for the day," he said.

Alison approached him. "Please! Won't you change your mind?"

"All I can do is speak to the Reverend. If he tells me it's OK, then it's OK." He opened the desk drawer, found a pencil and some paper, and pushed it to the edge of the desk. "Here. Write down the address where you're staying and I'll let you know."

"Who's the Reverend?" Terry looked hopeful. "Couldn't we talk to him ourselves?"

"He's taking a few weeks' vacation."

"Vacation!" Terry stared at him.

"Where did he go?" Eric asked.

"When will he be back?" Alison asked anxiously.

"Dunno where he went. He's on a fishing trip for a couple of weeks, maybe longer."

"A couple of weeks!" Eric couldn't have felt worse if he'd said *a couple of years.* "Isn't there anyone else we can talk to? Doesn't he have someone in charge while he's away?"

"Oh, sure. There's someone else to look after the Sunday services and all that, but Reverend Hardy is the only one knows about the cemetery. He's the one hired me and he's the only one to talk to. So write down your address and I'll let you know soon as I can get hold of him."

With a glance of despair at Alison and Eric, Terry wrote on the paper. "I'm putting the phone number here, too," he told Al. "That way you can call us the minute you know."

Al pulled out a large, round pocket watch. "It's after six anyway." He hoisted himself from the chair. "Time I got home. Come along."

He ushered them to the front door, went outside with them, and locked the door with his key. They all stood and watched him as he went around the side of the cottage and disappeared among the trees.

"Is there another way out of here?" Alison asked Terry.

"The main parking lot's that way. But what do we do now?"

"What can we do?" Eric was bitterly disappointed. "Our heirlooms are down there and he won't let us get at them."

"Let's go back and tell Aunt Barbara and the others." Alison said gloomily. "Maybe they'll have some ideas."

They headed for the gate where they'd parked their car. "I warned you he'd let us find it for him, then keep it for himself," Terry complained.

"But he can't!" Alison said. "It's legally ours. We know where it is now. We have Scarab's letter and directions showing that we're telling the truth." She heaved a dejected sigh. "But I guess we'd have to get a lawyer and go to court to prove it, if it came to that."

"We don't want anyone else knowing about it," Terry

said. "Too many people know already. This graveyard will be crowded with people trying to steal it."

"Same thing if we went to the police and told them he was keeping stolen property," said Eric.

Alison pushed the gate open so they could go through. "The treasure wasn't exactly stolen from us directly. No, we don't want to do that. It would only confuse things."

Eric opened the car door for her while Terry went around to the driver's side. "Anyway, we don't want to involve Al with the police. He's just doing his job, I guess."

Terry started the motor. "He doesn't need to be so pigheaded about it. What harm could it do if we opened that tomb and got the stuff out and closed it all up again?" The motor roared and the car skidded a little on the dirt road as he turned it around.

Eric agreed. "It isn't like we were going to hurt anything. He made it sound as though we were robbing the graves or something."

"Well," Alison said, "either he's afraid we might do some damage there, or Terry's right about him. He wants to take it himself."

Eric stared at her. "You really think he would?"

"Greed makes people do strange things. He doesn't seem to be dishonest, but how can we tell what he might do?"

"Don't you think he would?" Terry asked him.

"Maybe." Eric thought it over. Al had taken them into the crypt and let them find the right tomb. He'd even confirmed that it was the right one. All the time they'd been looking, he hadn't mentioned anything about not letting them take the treasure if they found it. Then, when they were sure . . . "I suppose he could be thinking of stealing it," he said. "We can't rule that out."

Terry turned the car onto the main road. "So what do we do? He might have gone to get some friends to help him. They'll probably come back tonight and get it, and here we are, doing nothing about it!"

"If he does take our treasure tonight, we couldn't even prove it was ever there." Alison looked forlorn. "All we have is a couple of papers a hundred years old saying it was there, once."

"For that matter, we're not even sure it's still there ourselves," Eric said. "We won't know anything until we get that coffin open."

They fell into thoughtful silence, Eric thinking hard. There had to be some way to get into the crypt, open the sarcophagus, and find out if the treasure was there before Al could make it disappear. A picture rose in his mind of Al, seated on his lawn mower with a treasure chest mounted behind him, driving away. Then he remembered something. "That's it!" he said suddenly.

The car swerved a little as Terry jerked his head to see what was the matter.

"Listen!" Eric was bubbling over. "Remember how Al was using the lawn mower when we first got to the cemetery?"

"Sure." Alison looked puzzled.

"OK. He'd store that in his tool shed, wouldn't he? But he didn't put it away. I think he just forgot about it, with all that was going on."

"So?" Terry said. "He sure couldn't get it into the main room of the cottage. There are steps inside the front door, and besides, the room's too small."

"Then there has to be another door into the tool shed!" Alison said.

"There is," Eric grinned. "I saw it when he put away the lantern. A big, wide door. I just caught a glimpse of it, but I don't think it could have been locked. He wouldn't have locked it until he put the mower away."

"Wow!" Terry pulled the car to the side of the road and braked hard. "Let's get back there! That door to the crypt wasn't locked. It only had a bolt."

"We can't go back there without tools to open that

coffin," Eric pointed out. "Probably the only tools Al keeps are gardening tools."

"Yeah, we might need a chisel and hammer," Terry said. "How do you get one of those stone coffins open, anyway?"

"I'm not sure, but we'll find out."

"Hey, just a minute, here," Alison said loudly. "We can't go breaking into Al's cottage. It's against the law."

"We won't be breaking in if the door's open," Eric said, annoyed. "And all we want is to take what's legally ours. That's not against the law. Start the car, Terry, and let's go back to the house."

Alison frowned. "Well, we'd better tell Aunt Barbara and the others what we're planning to do."

"Sure, we can do that." Terry pulled the car onto the road again.

No one was in the house when they got back, but there was a note on the kitchen table.

> Dan and Nell came to take us all to an early dinner. We weren't sure when you'd be back, so we've gone with them. There are sandwiches in the fridge, and lemon pie.
> Love,
> Aunt Barbara

Terry slumped into a chair. "Why did they have to pick this time? Just when we finally have some big news!"

"Maybe we should wait for them." Alison took a huge plate of sandwiches from the refrigerator and set them on the table.

"We can't," Eric objected. "Al might be back there right now, taking the treasure out."

"But we're not sure of that."

"We can't take any chances," Terry reminded her.

"Those heirlooms belong to us and we've worked hard to find them," Eric said. "We aren't going to do any damage to that cottage or the crypt or the coffin. We won't break into the cottage either. If the tool shed door turns out to be locked, we'll just have to think of something else. We're not committing any crime."

"Well . . . OK. But we'd better leave a note for the others to tell them where we are and what we're doing."

Eric stood up. "Why don't you write it, while Terry and I find some tools?"

"Aren't you going to eat something?" She looked up at them.

"I'm not very hungry." Eric grabbed a sandwich. "Come on, Terry."

Terry took one of the sandwiches and together they went to the garage to find tools they thought they would need. They were putting them in a canvas bag and setting them into the trunk of the De Soto when Alison found them. She carried a flashlight.

"Did you leave the note?" Terry asked her.

She nodded.

"Then let's go," Eric said.

Although they'd tried to hurry, it had taken them more than an hour to find the tools and a large canvas bag that would hold them as well as the treasure. It was after eight by the time they got back to the cemetery. They got the bag of tools out of the trunk, and Terry carried it as they walked toward the cottage. Eric's senses were alert for signs of anyone who might be watching them, but there was no one in sight. His nerves tingled as the three of them approached the cottage and he remembered the ghost they'd seen there.

They went around the side and heard the door to the tool shed creaking before they saw it, swaying slightly in the breeze.

"I thought so!" Eric was pleased with his power of deduction. "Al forgot to lock it."

"And he hasn't been back." Alison switched on the flashlight she carried and they went inside. She played the beam around the shed. "There's the lantern, right beside the other door."

Eric went toward the inside door with sudden apprehension. He couldn't remember if Al had locked that one or not. He tried the handle, turned it easily, and pushed it open.

They all went into the cottage.

He pushed the bolt back with no trouble and opened the door to the crypt. "Wait till I get the lantern," he said, taking it from its shelf and lighting it.

"This seems almost too easy," Terry said nervously.

Eric guided their way down the stairs, holding the lantern high, already catching the moldy scent of the crypt below. He could feel a trickle of sweat on his forehead and realized he was more nervous that he'd thought. The others, he knew, must be just as nervous. At the bottom, they all stopped and glanced uneasily around.

"This way," Eric said.

The silence was intense. The only sounds were the hissing of the lantern and the faint scuffling of their feet on the earthen floor. Eric jumped when the tools in Terry's bag clanked suddenly, and Alison gasped. Now the sarcophagus was in front of them and he could see the faint letters, *Stella Maris,* engraved on the top. They all examined it to see how it might be opened.

"Maybe this top comes off," Terry suggested.

Holding the lantern, Eric walked around it. The top was a heavy marble slab that would be difficult to lift, but at the front of the sarcophagus he cold see a thin crack under it. "Let's try the pry bar here," he said.

Terry took it from the bag and pushed the tapered end into the crack, while Eric felt sudden reluctance. Did they really want to open this? Suppose there was a body in it? But he handed the lantern to Alison and grasped the bar along with Terry. Together they pushed down as hard as they could. The coffin lid didn't budge. When they stopped to gather their strength, Eric took another look at the front of the coffin.

"Maybe this whole front comes off," he said. "It looks as though it's fitted into the rest of the coffin. Let's try pushing up on the bar, instead."

They strained, and in a moment Eric could feel the stone front of the sarcophagus moving slightly. "It's coming!" Excitement flooded through him. They'd see their treasure at last!

"Oh, I hope it isn't a body." Alison breathed.

The stone moved with a grating sound of complaint. The opening was an inch wide now. Two inches. Terry stopped to catch his breath, and Eric let go of the pry bar. He wedged all his fingers into the opening and yanked. The heavy stone front came down suddenly, sending him off balance. He bumped hard into something behind him and heard Alison exclaim before there was the sound of breaking glass and the light went out.

15 • The Treasure

"Ouch!" Alison cried out. "Eric! That hurt!"

"You OK?" He couldn't see her in this darkness.

Her voice was close to his ear, a moan of distress. "You pushed me right into this other coffin! Caught me in the middle of my back."

She hadn't broken any bones, then. Only the lantern. Just when they were going to see the treasure. "What were you standing right behind me for anyway?" he demanded.

"So you could see inside the coffin. Why do you think?"

"Let's get some light," Terry said. "Didn't you bring a flashlight, Alison?"

"Yes." She sounded doubtful.

"Well then, turn it on."

"I . . . I left it over there."

"Over where?" Eric tried to stay calm, but he was obsessed with an urgent desire to see into that coffin. Why had this happened just at this moment? Sure, he was the one who'd made her lose her grip on the lantern, but she could have taken better care of it.

"It's on top of one of these slabs. I just set it down so I could hold the lantern for you and now I'm not sure . . ."

"OK," Eric sighed. "Terry, feel around to your right and I'll go left."

"It's not far away," Alison said. "Maybe I can find it." She bumped into Eric. "Sorry. It's so black in here."

"Stay where you are," Eric told her. "There's no use all of us doing this. We'll find it." But the darkness in the crypt was complete, and it was hard to tell where he was in relation to the tomb they'd opened. The stone coffins all felt the same. He gripped the edge of one and leaned across it, spreading his hands over the surface carefully so as not to knock the flashlight off if he should touch it.

"You sure you didn't put it on the floor?" Terry asked, a few feet away.

"Pretty sure," Alison said. "But I wasn't really thinking about where I was putting it. I just wanted to see that coffin opened."

"Great," Eric muttered, moving his feet more carefully now toward the next sarcophagus.

"I'm right in front of this opening," Alison said. "I could get down and feel around inside . . ."

"I'd wait for a light," Terry said. "Maybe there's a body inside."

"Ooooh!" There was a shocked silence, then Alison spoke again. "Well, hurry up and find that flashlight. This place is creepy."

Eric agreed with her. It was bad enough in here when he could see, but now it was frightening. The airlessness and the smell of molding earth seemed stronger, the closed-in silence overwhelming. He leaned over the edge of another coffin and moved his hands over the top.

And then he heard the sound. It came from the top of the staircase. The sound of feet on the wooden steps, moving slowly. He froze.

"What's that?" Terry hissed through the darkness.

"Someone's coming!" Alison whispered.

Eric was cold with fear. Without thinking, he crouched

down beside the coffin, staring through the blackness in the direction of the sound. Was it Al? Whoever it was seemed to be alone and moving cautiously. Now he could see a glow of light. His heart pounded. The faint, whispering footsteps stopped. The glow wavered unevenly. There was an eerie, unearthly silence. Eric waited, hardly breathing. Time seemed to shudder to a stop.

Alison made a sudden sound of surprise. "Here it is! I found it!" Then a ray of light shone through the crypt. Eric jerked his head around into the beam of the flashlight. For a moment it blinded him, before Alison swung it toward the stairs.

"Who's there?" she called out.

Eric stood up. The flashlight beam wasn't strong enough to illuminate the stairs clearly, but he couldn't see anyone there.

"Al? Is that you?" She called again.

There was no answer . . . no sound. They waited another moment, then Alison spoke once more, her voice shaking now. "Didn't you guys hear what I did? Footsteps up there?"

"Yeah," Terry said. "See anyone?"

"No." Eric forced himself to go to the bottom of the staircase. "Alison, come on over here."

She followed, and they shone the flashlight up the steps. There was no one there.

"But I saw a light," she said. "It was sort of a glow," she broke off with a gasp.

"The ghost?" Terry quavered.

Eric wiped the sweat from his forehead. "Let's get the treasure and get out of here."

"Maybe we should go upstairs and take a look, just to be sure," Terry said.

Eric turned back toward the tomb marked *Stella Maris*. "If it was really the ghost, I don't want to see it again. If it was Al, he knows we're down here by now."

Alison followed Eric. "And if it's anyone else, we don't want to see them either."

Eric was still shivering, but only partly from fear. The excitement inside him was just as strong.

Now they were all standing in front of the dark opening in the coffin. Suddenly, Eric felt a strange reluctance. Of course the treasure would be there, he told himself. But if it was a body? Or what if the treasure wasn't there?

"Hurry!" Alison shoved the flashlight into his hands.

His fingers closed around it. He shone the beam an inch into the opening, seeing only bare stone. Then he was down on his knees, shining the light inside the tomb.

The coffin was empty.

He blinked and looked again. The walls seemed to lurch and tip before his eyes. He shone the light desperately around.

"What's there?" Alison leaned over his shoulder and Terry crouched beside him.

"Nothing." Eric heard the mournful word echoing around the inside of the tomb.

"Nothing?" Terry's hand grabbed for the flashlight. "Let me see." Eric's limp fingers let it go, and he waited numbly while Terry shone it around the walls. He couldn't believe this! His head was reeling. After all his hopes and dreams . . .

"Well?" Alison pushed at his shoulder impatiently, trying to see inside.

"Nothing!" Terry sat back on his heels.

"There's got to be!" Alison hissed. "Give me the flashlight. Maybe there's a false bottom in it." She took the light and leaned in front of Terry, pushing her fingers around the coffin floor.

A false bottom? Eric gauged the height of the inside from the floor. Could it be possible?

Alison made an excited sound. Her fingers were scrabbling underneath the little rim of the opening, and now she was pulling something out, holding it up into the light.

The light flashed against gold. It was a coin, about an inch across.

"Look at this!" Alison sighed. "It's beautiful."

"Then the treasure *was* here!" Eric took the coin from her and turned it over. The date looked like 1781, though they couldn't read it well, and it also said *George III, Rex.* "This was part of it."

"Can I see it?" Terry held out his hand. Alison and Eric stood up. She held the light while Terry looked at the coin. When he handed it back to her, his face was tight with anger. "Al! He got the rest of the stuff then."

"Wait," Eric said hopefully. "Maybe there *is* a false bottom. Where's the pry bar?"

Terry picked it up from the floor where Eric had dropped it. Then he inserted the end of the bar just under the floor of the coffin, but although they pushed on it as hard as they could, it didn't move. At last they had to give up, Eric wiping his moist face with the back of his hand.

"There's no false bottom," Terry said. "Al got here before we did."

They looked at each other hopelessly.

"We'd better get out of here," Alison said. "There's nothing more we can do."

"At least we got something back." Terry pushed the crowbar back into the canvas bag and hefted it. "Too bad this bag has to go home empty."

Eric knew how he must feel. And even though they'd found the coin, how many other valuables had there been? Was Al sifting through them this very moment? "We'll find the rest of the treasure, too." he told Terry. "Somehow. Some way. We'll find it."

"Yeah." Terry's voice was flat, without hope. "We'd better close up the coffin before we go."

They replaced the front of the sarcophagus, finding that

it fit easily into place, and then they followed Alison toward the staircase.

"Let's try to be quiet," she warned. "There might be somebody waiting up there."

Eric had almost forgotten those footsteps they'd heard, and the glow they'd seen. He slid his foot on the first step. "Want me to go first?"

Alison handed him the light and moved quietly behind him. With Terry following closely, they crept up the stairs.

Eric held his hand over the light so that it illuminated only the step above the one he was on. Every now and then he looked upward to the head of the stairs, but could see nothing. Was someone waiting there in the darkness?

When they had nearly reached the top, he let the beam flood the doorway. No one was there, or at least no one was visible. At the top step he gestured for them to wait as he poked his head and the light through the doorway. All he could see was the open door to the tool shed, the closed door in front of him that would be the bathroom, and Al's empty chair and cluttered desk.

"OK," he told the others. "Come on."

They followed him into the main room while he flashed the beam around, seeing no one. Then he pushed the door of the tool shed all the way back and looked in there. It was empty, the big outside door still slightly ajar.

"Let's split!" Terry said over his shoulder.

They went through the open door and outside into the soft, blue dusk. Eric shone the light around here, too, but saw only the trees.

Alison leaned against the wall of the cottage and took deep breaths. "Someone got here before us, after all," she said sadly.

"Yeah. We weren't fast enough," Terry muttered. "Al must have raced back here the minute we left today."

Eric felt exhausted. He, too, leaned against the rough wall and shoved his hands into his pockets. "That doesn't make sense, though," he said. "If Al came back here after we left, why did he leave this tool shed door open?"

"He probably didn't even notice it," Terry said.

"He'd have to see it if he wanted to get the lantern to take to the crypt. But the lantern and his flashlight were both there."

"He could have brought another light. Don't forget, he'd have to have help, wouldn't he? He couldn't carry all that stuff up the stairs by himself. Maybe whoever he brought with him had a light, so they wouldn't need another one."

"It's possible." Eric frowned, wondering.

"Sure," Terry said. "He'd hurry back because he figured we'd do just what we did. Maybe he was still here when we got here. Those footsteps . . ." He looked around uneasily. "Let's go home."

"OK." Eric led the way around to the front of the cottage and found the path. He was walking quickly alone, a little ahead of Alison and Terry, when he heard Alison's shriek.

He whirled around.

A greenish glow shone among the trees they had just passed, and as they stood staring, the ghostly figure of the pirate moved into sight.

16 • A Strange Message

Fear and shock turned Eric's body to lead, unable to move as he stared at the ghost among the trees, perhaps fifty feet away from them.

Neither Alison nor Terry moved, either. They could only watch as the figure put his hands on his hips and grinned at them—a mocking, sardonic smile. He stood this way for a moment, nodding his head, the plume on his hat fluttering. He waved his hand in a gesture Eric remembered, and the huge ring he wore glittered. "The treasure . . . is . . . mine!" he said, his voice a hollow baritone.

Eric's breath caught in his throat. Chills coursed through him. With an effort, he moved his hands, swung the flashlight up, and pointed it toward the ghost. But already the figure had turned away and was melting into the darkness.

"Come on!" Terry shouted, running toward the place it had been. Eric, too, was in motion now, his body freed from its initial shock.

"Over there!" Alison screamed to them, pointing.

They both changed their course, running past the front of the cottage toward the graveyard. But Eric could see only the gravestones shimmering white in the darkness; only the branches swaying, light catching on their leaves. He stopped and played the beam of the flashlight around. "Where?" he called to her.

"I saw something glowing over that way," she shouted.

Terry stopped too, and looked around. "I don't see a thing!"

Alison caught up with them, a bit out of breath. "It was right over here, that horrible greenish glow."

Eric swung the light over the gravestones, then back toward the cottage, but there was nothing. "It's gone."

"Let's take a look over where he was, then," Alison said.

They searched around the cottage and among the trees, half afraid of seeing the frightening figure again, staying close together and speaking in low voices, but there was no ghost here now. Finally they gave up and took the path back to their car.

"He just disappeared!" Alison said.

"What's so strange about that?" Terry said. "All ghosts just appear and disappear, don't they?"

"But I don't believe in ghosts. Not even now. It's got to be somebody dressed up to look like the pirate."

"It couldn't be Al," Terry said. "It didn't look like him at all."

"It didn't look like anybody we know," Eric agreed. "but with that beard and that hat pulled down over his eyes, how could we tell?"

"Al doesn't move that fast," Terry said.

"Well," Eric said, "if it's somebody pretending to be a ghost, what's he doing it for? Why did he say 'the treasure is mine?'"

"Trying to scare us away from the treasure, obviously." Alison pushed open the gate.

"But he didn't scare us away. He didn't appear until after we'd opened the coffin." Eric got into the car after her.

"That's true," Alison said thoughtfully. "It could have been him on the stairs when we were in the crypt, but nobody knew we'd be there, except our families, and maybe Al."

"And if Al got the treasure out of the crypt," Terry said, climbing in the driver's seat, "he wouldn't bother to pretend to be a ghost and try to scare us away."

"Even if it *was* a real ghost," Eric said, "he'd be wrong. The treasure isn't *all* his. You still have the coin, don't you, Alison?"

"Right here in my purse."

"Maybe he meant it *used* to be his," Terry said. "Didn't he say in his letter that his soul would be in torment until we got it back?" He drove carefully down the dirt road.

"Why didn't he come all the way down into the crypt?" Alison said. "He could have scared us even better down there, if that's what he wanted to do."

"He didn't know we were there," Terry said. "Remember? That was after the lantern got broken and we couldn't find the flashlight."

"You mean he couldn't see us in the dark?" Alison scoffed. "I thought ghosts could see anywhere, didn't you, Eric?"

Eric tried to follow their reasoning, but he was too tired to really think straight. "Right now all I can think of is a nice thick steak. Maybe two."

"I'm for that!" Terry said warmly. "With baked potatoes and a hot fudge sundae for dessert."

"There were only sandwiches in the fridge," Alison said with regret.

"We'd better go home, anyway," Terry said. "If Aunt Barbara's back, she'll be worried about us. And they'll all want to know what happened."

At the house, they found no one around and Alison's note still on the table in the kitchen. They brought out the rest of the sandwiches and pie, and it wasn't until they had eaten all of it that Eric felt renewed enough to face their dilemma again. He leaned back on the kitchen chair and held out his hand toward Alison. "Let me see the coin again, will you?"

She picked up the purse she'd deposited on the floor beside her, took it out, and gave it to him. He examined it closely in the light. The date and the other features were worn and difficult to make out. "Still, it's beautiful," he said. "I wonder what the rest of the treasure was like?"

"Chances are we'll never know now," Terry said sadly. "Unless Al decides to confess."

"And we can't just go to the cemetery and tell him we suspect him," Alison said.

Eric nodded. "But we will have to tell him we opened the coffin. We smashed up his kerosene lantern, remember? So we can bring him another one, and casually mention that the treasure had been stolen before we got there."

"I'm going to have a hard time of being casual with him," Terry frowned. "Anyway, he's not going to tell us. I think we should go to the police now."

"The police?" Aunt Barbara was in the doorway with James behind her wheelchair. "Why do you want to go to the police?"

They all looked up to greet the two of them, and Terry asked, "Didn't Aunt Nell and Uncle Dan come with you?"

"No. They brought us home more than an hour ago, then left for some meeting. James and I went out again to pick up a few groceries."

"Then you saw my note?" Alison said.

"Yes. When they brought us home, we were all hoping you'd be here. We all read the note, and I must say that if you'd been here then, we would have told you not to go into that crypt. It wasn't the right thing to do at all—that is, if I got the right meaning out of what you wrote, Alison. You were breaking into church property!"

She nodded, looking a bit shamefaced. "It seemed the only thing to do at the time. We thought it would be all right."

"We didn't damage anything there," Terry said. In a lower voice, he added, "Except for breaking the lantern."

"Well." Aunt Barbara looked at each of them. "Perhaps you'd best tell us the whole story."

"Find the treasure?" James showed his rusty smile and leaned against the kitchen counter.

"Just this one piece." Eric got up to show them the coin.

James's smile dissolved into a look of surprise. "You found that? Is it real? There really is a treasure?"

Aunt Barbara turned it over in her hands, looking at it with admiration. For a long moment she said nothing. Then she looked up, her face glowing. "It's part of our past. Just think! A piece of family history, right here in my hand. It's exquisite!"

"Where'd you find it? In that crypt?" James examined the coin his mother handed him.

They told their story together. To Eric, it was like reliving the night's experiences. He wondered if Terry and Alison were as exhausted as he was. Terry sounded tired as he told of Scarab's ghost, and how they'd had enough presence of mind this time to chase it.

"You take too many chances!" Aunt Barbara looked frightened. "How do you know what might have happened to you, chasing a ghost? There are many things in this world we don't understand. It's better to leave them alone."

"Then you think it's really Scarab's ghost?" Alison asked her. "Not just somebody trying to scare us?"

Aunt Barbara shook her head emphatically. "My dear! Who would try to scare you away from a treasure that isn't there?"

"But if it's a person, he might not have known the treasure wasn't there," Eric said. "Maybe he's waiting for us to find it, then he'll try to take it from us."

"That's an idea, Eric!" Alison was enthused. "This person, whoever he is, might know about the treasure but not where it is. It's only been us here in this room, Dan, Nell, and Al who saw both halves of the directions put together. So maybe this person is following us, waiting until we find it, and then he'll try to step in and take it."

James shook his head doubtfully. "You only saw him in the cemetery. Right?"

"Not exactly," Terry said. "We think he's the one who started down the stairs to the crypt and then went back up again."

"But you only see him near the churchyard where he's buried, so it must be the ghost of Scarab." James spoke with the finality of a man whose mind is made up.

"Yes," Aunt Barbara agreed. "Scarab was a cruel and heartless pirate—a tormented soul. I'd be scared to death if I saw him! I certainly wouldn't chase him, and I don't think you should go anywhere near him."

"Well, we have to go back to the cemetery once more," Terry said. "We have to find out if Al was the one who took the treasure. I think he was."

"Where does he live?" Aunt Barbara asked. "It might be best to go to his house. Maybe he has it there."

Terry shrugged. "I don't know. We didn't even find out his last name, did we?" He looked at Eric.

"No. But we have to replace his lantern, so we'll take it to his cottage in the cemetery. But there's nothing more we can do. We have no way of knowing where the treasure is now."

"We've come to a dead end," Alison added.

Aunt Barbara looked distressed. "What were you saying about the police?"

Terry answered her. "I think we should go to the police now and tell them Al stole our property."

"But Al could tell them you broke into the church crypt and opened a coffin without permission." She smiled at them. "You all look worn out. Why don't you go to bed now and we can phone Dan and Nell in the morning. Maybe someone will come up with an idea."

Eric had been so tired he slept late the next morning, and the sun was high by the time he went down for breakfast. Only Alison was in the kitchen, making toast and hot chocolate.

"Everyone else has eaten already," she told him.

"Where are they?" he took the mugs of hot chocolate to the table and sat down.

"Terry's helping Aunt Barbara fold some laundry. James is in his workshop." She poured two bowls of cereal. "Everybody's feeling discouraged this morning, including me."

"Yeah. Me, too." Eric poured milk onto his cereal. "Looks like our treasure hunt has come to an end."

"Well, at least we found the gold coin."

She nodded. "But that just makes me feel worse. We found one coin, but none of our family heirlooms or the Roberts's."

Three chimes sounded. Eric looked up. "What's that?"

"The doorbell?" Alison listened.

The chimes sounded again.

"Wonder if anyone else heard it?" Eric got up. "I'll answer it."

He went along the empty hall to the front door, and opened it. The young man who stood outside seemed to be about twenty, dressed in jeans and a worn shirt with rolled-up sleeves. Behind him, on the driveway, a black pickup truck with rusted fenders waited, its motor throbbing.

"Can I speak to Eric Thorne?" the man said.

127

"I'm Eric Thorne." He didn't recognize this man. Why was he asking for him?

"This is for you." The man reached into the pocket of his frayed shirt, pulled out a folded piece of paper and handed it to him.

Puzzled, Eric unfolded the paper. There was only a name and address written on it in shaky, uneven handwriting.

Alphonse Richard
1811 Appletree Lane
Monterey

"Who is this?" Eric asked.

"A guy who wants to see you. He said to be sure to come alone. Six-thirty today."

Al, Eric thought. It has to be. "What does he want with me?" he asked.

The man shrugged. "I don't know. He lives up the street from me. Gave me ten bucks to drive here and hand this to you personally." He peered at Eric under ragged black eyebrows. "OK? Can I tell him you'll be there? Alone?"

"Well . . . all right. But can't you give me any information at all?"

"'Fraid not. That's all I know." The man turned and started down the front step, then stopped and turned back. "You'll be sure to be alone? I have to tell him."

Eric nodded. "Yes, I'll come alone." He went back inside the house, staring at the paper in his hand, and closed the door behind him.

It was then the name on the paper seemed to jump out at him. *Richard.*

That was Scarab's real name!

17 • The Meeting

They all gathered in the glass-walled living room. Nell and Dan had driven over that morning to hear about the events in the cemetery, and everyone was as puzzled over the mysterious summons as Eric had been.

"The address is only a few blocks from where we live, but I don't know this man," Dan said. He shook his head. "I think you might be right, Eric. The name Richard—it isn't as common a name as Richards, for instance. This man might be some relative of Hippolyte Richard."

"But how would he know you, Eric?" Nell asked. "And where you're staying?"

Eric nodded. "We gave him our address when we met him at the cemetery. And he knows our names." Thinking about it, Eric remembered how Al had stared at him when he'd first introduced himself. "But why would he want to see *me?* Alone?"

Terry looked triumphant. "I must be right. He's got the treasure. Now he's probably had a change of heart and decided to confess."

"Then why not confess to all three of us?" Eric shook his head. "I don't think that's why he was so curious about why we wanted to see the grave. He knew we weren't relatives. I wonder why he didn't tell us?"

Aunt Barbara smoothed back her graying curls. "This Al seems to be mysterious. But if he's really related to Scarab, I imagine he can tell you something about the treasure."

"Sure," Terry said sourly. "Like what he's bought with it."

"But then, why Eric alone?" Nell said. "It would seem more likely he'd want all three of them there, together."

James gave a short, mirthless laugh. "Maybe he wants to hassle you about it one at a time." He stood up and winked at Eric. "Good luck!"

"Are you going to work?" Terry asked him.

"Not today. I finished the Studebaker. Today I'm going to borrow a boat. Been curious to see that cavern under the house."

"You could use ours," Dan told him. "It's still down there, isn't it, Terry?"

"We haven't had much chance to bring it back, with all this excitement."

"That's all right," Dan said. "We weren't planning to use it right away. Would you like to borrow it, James?"

"No. Thanks. My friend has one. He's going to come with me. We'll be doing a little fishing, too."

Aunt Barbara watched him go, looking anxious. "Well, I hope he doesn't go exploring all those caves down there. They go way back under the rock. Goodness knows what might be in some of them!"

Dan smiled at her. "He'll be fine, Barbara. I'm more worried about Eric, here, and his meeting with this mysterious Mr. Richard." He handed the paper back to Eric. "If he's angry about your breaking into church property, he's well within his rights, you know. If I can give you some advice, just listen to what he has to say and don't argue with him."

Eric had no intention of arguing with the old caretaker. "But I don't think that's why he wants to see me. If he wanted to complain, why not phone us? Or come here himself?"

"Who knows?" Dan and Nell exchanged puzzled glances.

"Anyhow, why don't you drive home to Monterey with us?" Nell asked him. "You could walk from our house."

"I can drive him, Aunt Nell," Terry said. "Alison and I can take him and wait at your house until he's seen this guy. Then we can hear what happened as soon as he gets back to your house. OK?"

"That way you won't have to drive me back," Eric said.

Early that evening, Terry drove the De Soto to Monterey and deposited Eric a block away from Appletree Lane.

"We'll be waiting to hear what's going on," Alison told him as they left. "Hope it's something about the treasure."

"Me too." Eric waved to them, then began walking.

Appletree Lane was a short street of older homes and judging from the people he saw on the porches and lawns, older inhabitants. Number 1811 was a small blue house with a Spanish tile roof and an adobe wall around the flower garden in front. Eric pushed open the wrought-iron gate and went up the path to the tiny, closed-in porch.

The door opened before he could ring the bell. Al stood neatly dressed in a white shirt, open at the collar, and brown pants. His gray hair was slicked back from his wrinkled forehead, and he looked at Eric with something like relief on his face.

"Glad to see you. Come on in."

The house was dim and cool, and smelled of the roses Eric had seen growing in profusion outside. He followed Al through a small living room filled with heavy antique furniture. Framed photographs were everywhere—on the mantel over the fireplace, the piano in the corner, the end tables. The caretaker led him to a chair.

"My family." Al waved to the pictures. "Most of them grandchildren and great-grandchildren. Got seven great-grandchildren. Sit down."

Eric sank into the cushion of the overstuffed chair Al indicated and tried to look interested in the pictures, hiding his uneasiness with what he hoped was a polite smile.

"Youngest is only three months old," Al said. "Lives in Oregon now." He sat on a bentwood rocker across from Eric. "Guess you were surprised to get my note."

"I didn't know your name was Alphonse Richard," Eric said. "Are you any relation to Scarab?"

"I'm his great-grandson. He died twenty years before I was born. From what my grandmother told me about him, he was a good father and a good husband—no matter what else he did."

"But you never said anything about it when you took us to his grave."

"Like I told you, not many people knew he was a pirate. Why should I tell you that I'm the great-grandson of the man who robbed your families?" Al rocked his chair rhythmically. "I guess information like that is best kept secret, even though by this time, it doesn't matter much."

"Sure," Eric said. "It's nobody's business anyway. All we had to know was how to find the treasure he left for us."

Al nodded. "I took you where you wanted to go. That was as much as I could do for you." He reached for a pipe on the table next to him and began to fill it, tamping the tobacco slowly.

Eric felt more uneasy than ever and wished Al would say something; tell him why he was here. Did he know they'd opened the coffin last night? Or was he going to confess that he'd taken the treasure out before they got there? Finally, the question burst out of him. "Why did you ask me to come here?"

"I'm coming to that." Al looked up, his faded blue eyes

on Eric's. "But first, tell me where you got the name 'Eric.'"

"My name?" This was the last thing he'd expected. "I . . . my dad told me a lot of Thornes were named Eric."

"I see. But you have a letter from Scarab, you said."

"Yes, but it's back at the house. We showed you the two halves of the directions, though."

Al nodded. "You say your father had one half, and you found the other?"

"That's right. We found it in some clothing that must have belonged to John Roberts."

"I don't know that name."

"He was Terry's ancestor. The one on the ship with Eric Thorne." Why didn't he get to the point? "Is this something about the treasure?"

"Could be," Al said. "I'm not sure."

"Then what?" But Eric knew there was no use trying to pry the information from him. Obviously something was weighing on his mind.

Al got up from his chair, went to the piano, and picked up one of the framed photographs there. He brought it back and handed it to Eric. "This is my grandmother," he said. "She's been gone for over fifty years. This was taken in 1895."

Eric looked at the soft features, the wavy hair, the dangling earrings. The woman was middle-aged and attractive, wearing a long, flowing gown decorated with feathers. "She's pretty," was all he could think of to say until an idea hit him. "Do you have any pictures of your great-grandfather?"

"Why?" Al looked at him sharply.

"We saw his ghost in the cemetery again last night. Whatever it is, someone wants us to think it's his ghost. If I could see a picture of him, I'd . . ." Eric broke off, seeing Al's startled expression. What had he been thinking of? He'd let it slip! He hadn't been going to tell Al now—not before he knew why he'd been summoned here. Well, it was too late now.

Al yanked the picture out of his hands. "Why were you in the cemetery last night?"

"We had to find out what was in that coffin. You left the door to your tool shed open, so we went down to the crypt and opened it."

The old caretaker turned and went back to the piano, setting the picture on it. Eric wished he could see his face. Would he show guilt if he'd been the one who took their treasure? Or would there only be anger?

It was a moment before Al turned. His face was expressionless, his voice cool. "So you went ahead in spite of what I said? Well, what did you find?"

"The tomb was empty, except for one gold coin."

Al sat down and puffed on his pipe, his face thoughtful.

"We didn't do any damage," Eric told him uneasily. "Except we broke your kerosene lamp. It was an accident. We'll replace it."

He waved his hand as though this was of no consequence. "You say you saw a ghost? Scarab's ghost?"

"Yes. When we came outside again it was dark, and the ghost was there. I thought if you had a picture of your great-grandfather, I might be able to tell if it was really his ghost we saw."

Al waved his hand again, this time toward the back of the room. "There's only a painting. It's very old. It's been hanging over there ever since I can remember."

Eric got up and went in the direction Al had pointed, looking at the assortment of photographs hanging in a line on the wall. And there it was. The painting of a broad-shouldered man on horseback. But he didn't look like a pirate. He wore a long-sleeved brown shirt and brown pants in the style of the nineteenth century. His hair was dark and curly, brushed neatly back from his face. His beard was carefully trimmed. There was a scar on his

134

nose, and one of his front teeth was missing, but his smile was cheerful.

"Well?" Al said. "Is he the one you saw?"

"It's hard to tell." Eric was disappointed. "He wore this big hat and his clothes were a lot different." But now Eric noticed the hands, holding the horse's reins. "Wait a minute! It must have been Scarab! There's the emerald ring!"

Al hoisted himself from his rocker and came to stand beside Eric. "That ring gave him his pirate name. See? It's carved in the shape of the scarab beetle. My grandmother said he never took it off."

"Do you have it now?"

"No. I don't know what happened to it. Maybe he was buried wearing it." He scratched his head thoughtfully. "But if his ghost is haunting the cemetery, I've never seen it. Nobody else I know of has, either."

"And we've seen it twice. He only appears to us, then. This time he spoke to us. He said, 'The treasure is mine.'"

"I thought he told you in his letter the treasure was yours." The faded blue eyes searched Eric's face.

"I know. It doesn't make sense. None of it does. What happened to the treasure? Why was that coffin empty?" He shook his head, feeling as baffled as ever. But this might be the time to ask the burning question. He kept his voice and expression as casual as he could. "Do you have any idea, Al?"

The old caretaker didn't answer. He turned away and moved to an old-fashioned sideboard that stood against the wall. Then he opened the top drawer, pulled out a large manila envelope and searched through it, at last extracting a thick, white envelope. "Here," he said handing it to Eric. "This is why I wanted you to come here. Alone."

Eric stared at the writing on the envelope. There were two words: *Eric Thorne.* He looked at Al, bewildered. "This is for me? What is it?"

"Open it," Al said. "It's from my grandmother."

18 • Voice From the Past

"This letter is addressed to me!" Eric couldn't believe what he saw. "It's from your *grandmother?*"

"That's right. She made me promise to give it to you if you ever came here." Al turned away and went back to his rocking chair.

Eric followed, holding the letter with shaking fingers. He perched on the edge of the chair. "I don't understand. If your grandmother died fifty years ago, how could she know I'd come here?"

"All I know is before she died she told me, 'When Eric Thorne comes here, give him this. Don't let anyone but Eric Thorne have it.'" He rocked slowly, puffing on his pipe. "I remember it all so well. She died in this very house, in that bedroom . . ."

Eric turned the envelope in his hands, bewildered. It couldn't be meant for him. Should he open it? He felt like he was opening someone's else's mail. But Al had insisted. He slowly peeled the flap open, the old glue giving easily, and pulled out the papers that were inside.

It was a letter, written in a rounded, almost childlike, handwriting, and it was dated September 10, 1887.

Dear Eric Thorne,

After a long search I found the house where you once lived. The neighbors tell me you left several years ago to go east, to what address or even city they do not know. If you are reading this letter, you have done as I was sure you would. You have returned to claim what is yours.

The letter was meant for his ancestor, then. The Eric Thorne that had come here so long ago, from England. That made more sense, at least. Eric read on.

By now you know that Hippolyte Richard was once the pirate Scarab. I am his son's wife. Of his sins, you have learned. Of mine, I will tell you in hope that by this means I might right a wrong that had been done you. Hippolyte would wish it so. He meant to return to you what was rightfully yours, but I helped to spoil his plans. I have been foolish and misguided by John Roberts and his soft speeches. He has the heart of a stone.

Hippolyte died a year ago in March. For many years he disguised himself by dyeing his hair and wearing a beard so that none would perchance recognize him as Scarab. But upon his death, there was talk. How the truth came out I am still not certain. Perhaps Hippolyte himself let something slip to a friend in an unguarded moment. Be that as it may, John Roberts heard the talk that he once was a pirate, and attended the funeral to see my dead husband's face for himself. He must have followed us home to discover our whereabouts, but it was months before he appeared on our doorstep and insinuated himself into our house as a friend. I turned to him in his kindness, since I myself am a widow with four young children and nowhere else to find such comfort.

When he had convinced me completely of his good faith, he told me he knew that my husband had stolen his property and showed me the letter and the half sheet Hippolyte had sent him while on his deathbed.

I confess myself now to have been a fool. This old man treated me with such gentle generosity, I even gave him the scarab ring to show my gratitude. I let him tempt me with the idea that we could both share in the hidden treasure. Half was his, he told me, but the other half could be mine. He spoke of you, Eric Thorne, as a dishonest and selfish man, without morals or scruples, who came by your wealth in devious ways. I know now he lied, but at that time I let him convince me to tell him where Hippolyte had hidden your goods in the church crypt. Together we went there in the dead of night and removed it.

Eric looked up from the letter at Al, still rocking in his chair, his eyes half closed, apparently deep in his own thoughts. How could they have suspected him of taking the treasure? Eric felt a bit ashamed. He should have trusted his own feelings. Al was a nice old guy. Did he know what his grandmother had done? And why was she telling him all this, anyway? He went back to the letter.

Let me tell you, in truth, that I wanted your wealth not out of greed, but out of concern for the welfare of my fatherless children. I believed so fully in the goodness of John Roberts because he seemed to take such loving care of my children. This all stopped, however, once he had the treasure in his own hands. He took it all away and gave me nothing.

I could not confess the theft to the authorities. I would implicate myself if I did. And so, knowing where he lived in a small house on a cliff by the coast,

I went to beg him to keep his promise to me. I reminded him that I had steeped myself in sin on his account and now my children were left with nothing. He laughed at me. He boasted that he had hidden the treasure in a place it could never be found and that he himself would disappear as soon as his affairs were in order so that you, Eric, would never find him. His greatest fear was that you would come looking for him. He said that when you could not find him, and gave up your search, he would leave California and live like a king. His eldest son lives with him, and I believe this son has been instructed to tell you he knows nothing of his father's whereabouts or the other half of the paper telling where your wealth was hidden. This son is now building a larger house on the site of his father's.

Would she be talking about Aunt Barbara's house? It sounded like it—"on a cliff by the coast." Aunt Barbara had told them the house was built about the time this letter was written.

I believe John Roberts is hiding somewhere in that house. The only clue I have to the whereabouts of your goods are the words John Roberts boasted to me. "It is in the cave of the monster."

Eric shivered. Could that be one of those caves under the house? What kind of monster could be there? Would the treasure still be there, or had John gone away and taken it with him?

When you come with your half of the directions looking for John Roberts, do not believe whatever lies the son might tell you. And since it is now known that my husband was once Scarab, I feel sure you will come here if you cannot find John. I cannot wait here for you. In less than a week I must go away. But I will leave instructions that this letter is to be given to you. I pray it will guide you to recover the wealth that has been stolen from you. And I beg your forgiveness for that crime that I, in my weakness, helped John Roberts to commit.

Believe me, Sir, I am
Your faithful servant,
Hope Richard

Eric set the letter on his knee and smoothed the paper, trying to sort out his feelings. It had answered many questions, but left him with many more. Obviously the original Eric Thorne it was meant for had never received it. Had John Roberts taken the treasure away when Eric never appeared? Or could it be still in the cave?

"You've read it all?"

Eric looked up to see Al watching him curiously. "Yes. Your grandmother wrote it to my ancestor, the one who came on the ship Scarab pirated."

Al nodded. "I thought as much." He leaned forward, watching Eric's face. "Was it about the treasure you're looking for?"

"Yes. Didn't your grandmother tell you what she'd written?"

"No. She never said what was in it, or that she knew anything about your family's treasure."

Eric considered for a moment. Should he show the letter to Al? It was a personal confession, after all. How would he feel, reading his grandmother's admission that she was a thief?

Al seemed to know what he was thinking. "If my grandmother had wanted me to know what was in it, she would have told me. I don't want to read it. It's for you. But I have to admit I'm curious. Is there anything she said that you want to tell me?"

"It's mostly about our treasure and what happened to it. She knew who took it out of the crypt. It was taken to a place she called 'the cave of the monster.' Know where that might be?"

"Never heard of any place like that."

"Al, your grandmother said she had to go away someplace, and that's why she left this letter for Eric Thorne. But she must have come back. You said she died here, in this house. Didn't she want to tell all this to Eric Thorne herself?"

"When did she write the letter?"

Eric turned back to the first page. "September 10, 1887."

"That was long before I was born. See, she had to go to work after that. She went to San Francisco and became an actress on the stage. Sent money home regular so her kids would be taken care of." He puffed his pipe, a faraway look on his face. "Later she came back and lived with my father, and then me. She never forgot about Eric Thorne, though. She always thought that some day he'd come. And before she died, she gave me the letter. I didn't even know who Eric Thorne was, but I promised I'd give it to him if he ever came."

"In a way, he did." Eric stood up. "Thank you for giving me this letter, Al."

"I kept my promise. I feel good about that." Al pulled himself up from his chair and held out his hand to shake Eric's. "I hope it helps you."

"I hope so, too," Eric said as they went to the front door. "And don't forget, we still owe you one kerosene lantern."

"Maybe that'll teach you. Doing what you're not supposed to do never pays off." Al's high-pitched laugh followed Eric as he went down the path and though the gate.

Heading down Appletree Lane with the letter in his hand, Eric thought over Al's last words. His grandmother had done what she wasn't supposed to do, and John Roberts had stolen from her, in turn. How she must have hated him! So much that she tried to get revenge by writing this letter.

But now he had another problem. He'd have to show Terry's family the letter. It concerned them as much as it did him. Would they take John Roberts's guilt on themselves after such a long time? As he hurried along the sunlit street toward Dan and Nell's house, he wondered how the others in his own family would feel if it turned out that John Roberts had left California and spent their part of the inheritance. He didn't quite know how he'd feel about that, himself.

19 • A Difficult Decision

Alison finished reading the letter. "The more I think about this, the more I'm sure that cave has to be the one under the house."

The old car rolled smoothly along the coast highway, going back to the house on the cliff. Alison sat between Eric and Terry in the front seat, re-reading Hope Richard's letter, while Eric wished Terry could drive the car faster. He couldn't of course, since James had warned him against it, but traveling at forty miles an hour while everyone else passed them made him impatient.

"It all adds up, doesn't it? If John Roberts was hiding out, wouldn't that be the perfect place? And that trunk where we found his half of the directions. If he was living down there in one of those caves, wouldn't he keep his clothes there, too?"

"Hey, you could be right!" Terry seemed excited at the idea. "If Eric Thorne or the police came looking for him, they'd never even guess the caves were there. Nobody but the smugglers knew about it."

Eric thought it over. "It does make sense. If he hid in the cavern under the house, his son could have brought

143

him food and supplies. He could have even kept himself busy helping the smugglers." He could feel his own excitement mounting. The treasure might still be there, under the house somewhere. John Roberts would have stayed there until he was sure the coast was clear. How long? Six months, or a year? He looked at Terry. "How old do you figure John Roberts would have been in 1887?"

Alison answered first. "In her letter, Mrs. Richards calls him an old man."

Terry nodded. "We could figure it out. In 1850, when he came here, he already had a wife and kids. So he must have been in his thirties, at least."

"Could be," Eric said, "but people married younger in those days, didn't they? Let's say he was thirty. So if he was born in 1820, that would make him 67 in 1887. Chances are he was a few years younger."

"I guess you can be greedy no matter how old you are," Alison said. "Why are you worried about how old he was, Eric?"

"I was just thinking about how long he'd have to hide out in the cavern. It would be cold and damp down there."

"But if the secret passages were there," Terry said, "he could go back into the house that way any time he wanted to, except when people were around. Maybe he even spent the nights in the house."

Then Eric had another thought. "Even if he died in those caves," he said, discouraged again, "his son would have taken the treasure."

"If John told him where it was," Alison said.

Terry looked worried. "Don't tell me you want to give up the search, Eric? Just when we've got another clue?"

"No. I want to search the caves anyway. We can still use Dan and Nell's boat. That way we'd know for sure if the treasure's there or not." He looked at his sister. "How about you, Alison?"

"Well, I'm not too crazy about bumping into a monster."

"John Roberts probably just made that up," Terry said.

"Or it might just be a monster rock, or a monster stalactite," Eric added.

"Or a monster bat?" Alison laughed. "Sure. I want to hunt that treasure down until we find it or find out it's gone. Whichever."

Back at the house, they found Aunt Barbara and James having dinner in the glass-walled room, the sky behind them red with the setting sun.

"I never know when to expect you, so we didn't wait," she smiled at them. "But I've made plenty. Sit down."

"We had a bite to eat at Uncle Dan's," Terry said, eyeing the bowls of spaghetti and salad on the table. "But I'm still hungry."

"That looks delicious," Eric said.

"We didn't eat much." Alison seated herself next to James. "We were in a hurry to get back here and let you know what happened. And we stopped to buy a lantern to take to Al tomorrow."

James spoke without looking up from his food. "How'd you come out with the caretaker, Eric?"

Eric sat down and pulled the letter out of his pocket. "He turned out to be a really nice guy. Here, Aunt Barbara, why don't you read this out loud?"

She read the letter, exclaiming every now and then with surprise or dismay. When she finished, she shook her head sadly. "I never would have believed that one of our ancestors could have been so evil! Why, this poor woman should have gone straight to the police."

"But she helped him," Alison reminded her. "And her father-in-law stole our treasure in the first place. They'd arrest her."

"But she had all those poor little children." Aunt

Barbara sighed. "Oh, I know she was wrong, but I feel sorry for her."

Eric dug into his spaghetti. "Do you know anything about what happened to John Roberts? Did he leave the state?"

"I don't know. His son was my great-grandfather, you know, and I don't know much about him, either. I suppose we should keep better records of our family, but none of us have." She looked at Terry. "By the way, your mom phoned today to see how you were. I think you ought to call her back when you're through dinner."

Alison looked suddenly worried. "Eric, maybe we should call Dad, too. Just to let him know we're all right."

Eric nodded. "Aunt Barbara, do you know anything about this cave of the monster?"

"Doesn't that sound like an awful place? No, I've never heard of such a thing."

"Do you think it might be one of the caves under this house?" Alison asked.

She looked startled, then shook her head. "I'm sure it isn't there. Why, those caves go way back under the rock. I don't think anybody's ever been back there. And besides, it's dangerous." She looked to James. "What do you think?"

"Dunno. I went back there a little way today, but I didn't see any monsters." He buttered a piece of bread.

"But we're pretty sure that's where John Roberts hid out," Terry said, and went on to explain what they had talked about on the way home.

She only looked at them silently when he was finished. "So we thought we'd go and explore the rest of the cavern," Eric said. "At least we'll find out if the treasure's there or not."

"Well . . ." she smiled faintly. "I know how much this means to you. To all of you."

"Doesn't it mean something to you, too?" Terry said.

"Yes. Yes, I guess it does. Those are the heirlooms of

both our families, aren't they?" She twisted her fork absently in her hands. "And if you find it, our share will mean a lot to us, won't it, James? We'll have to turn some of it into cash, what with my medical expenses and this house, and all."

James nodded silently, watching her.

"When do you plan to go?" she asked.

"Tonight!" Terry looked around to see if Eric and Alison agreed.

Both of them did. "We want to go as soon as we can," Alison said.

"Tonight? That soon?" Aunt Barbara seemed flustered. "But it will be dark down there."

"It's always dark down there," Eric said. "The only light comes from the mouth of the cave, and that only shines in a little way."

"We'll take lights with us," Terry said. "We'll see as well that way as we would in the daytime."

She considered a moment before she spoke. "Well, all right. But I'll have to ask you to clean up the dinner dishes. I have another one of those awful headaches coming on. I can feel it starting. I'll just have to go and lie down."

"And I've got work to do." James got up from the table.

"That's OK," Alison said. "We'll take care of it."

"Thank you, my dear." Aunt Barbara smiled at all of them. "And do be sure to call your families, too, and ask them if you have their permission to go through those caves. After all, theirs is the final word."

When the dinner was finished, Eric, Alison, and Terry cleared away the dishes. Then while Terry phoned his parents, Eric helped Alison in the kitchen. They had everything done by the time Terry had made his call.

"My folks just wanted to know how we're doing," he said. "I told them what's been happening without going into all the details. They think we're doing a great job."

"Did they say it was OK to go to the caves tonight?" Alison dried her hands on a towel.

"My dad remembers the caves and he's heard about the smugglers. They just said to be careful, and they wished us good luck. I didn't mention the cave of the monster, just in case they wouldn't like that too much."

"Dad doesn't know anything about the caves or what they're like," Eric said. "It would only worry him if we try to describe them. Let's just give him a brief progress report and let him know we're fine."

"OK," Alison agreed.

Their tasks and phone calls took over an hour, so it was after nine o'clock by the time they were ready to use the hidden passage to get to the cavern below. Now they stood in the office in front of the sliding bookcase, and Alison was taking inventory of their supplies. "Each one of us has a light, right?"

"I've got a flashlight and extra batteries in my pocket." Eric held up the waterproof jacket he was carrying.

"And I'm bringing the kerosene lantern we bought for Al. It's just what we need," Terry said.

"Good. We all have warm jackets. Should we take any tools, in case we have to open the treasure chest?"

"That's really positive thinking," Eric told her, grinning. "Who knows what we'll run into? I've got my pocket knife, and there are probably tools in the boat, aren't there, Terry?"

"A tool kit. For emergency repairs. I think we have all we need." He smiled at Alison. "Except for a monster zapper."

"Very funny," she said sarcastically.

Eric was in no mood to waste time. He pushed the shelf of books that opened the panel. "Come on," he said. "Let's go."

20 • The Cave of the Monster

The boat waited, bobbing on the swell, moored where they'd left it by the ledge at the bottom of the ladder.

Eric and Alison climbed in while Terry unfastened the bowline, then Eric held the boat at the ledge until he had boarded.

The cavern was in darkness except for the faint light still coming in through the entrance. Eric could hear the now familiar tinkling of water, the lapping and rushing of the sea coursing through the channels, and the other faint, unknown noises that echoed through the caves.

"Still smells like dead fish down here," Alison remarked.

Terry started the motor, and as soon as it was going he lit the kerosene lantern and handed it to Eric, sitting next to him. In the seat behind, Alison played her flashlight beam toward the port side. It wasn't long until they saw the first channel branching off to their left.

"It's too narrow to navigate," Terry said.

Eric could see that it was. He moved the light over the flat surface of rock that loomed before them and saw two more streams—one that narrowed in the distance, the other curving around a rocky outcropping. This was the only way they could go. He signaled to Terry, who was already turning the boat slowly around the rocks.

Perhaps it was because of the echoes in here, but it sounded to Eric as though another boat traveled the course with them. He looked behind them, but his light showed nothing there. The echoes were playing tricks.

"Look!" Alison shouted.

Stalactites and stalagmites gleamed like ice in her flashlight beam, in a glittering cavern where a waterfall trickled down the white wall. It was beautiful and eerie, but Eric could only glance at it before he had to turn back guiding the boat's path with his lantern. It was illuminating a low arch ahead, now, that they would have to go under. He tried to gauge if the boat would make it.

"I think it's OK," Terry said in a tight voice. Eric held his breath, but they went under it with room to spare.

Their channel narrowed and widened again, and they went between rocky cliffs where a labyrinth of caves could be seen, some high up in the rocks, some nearly submerged. They shined their lights at them as they passed, sometimes seeing small things scurrying, and once a pair of tiny eyes shining at them. Rats, and maybe other creatures.

Now their channel made another turn and a low, narrow bridge of rock spanned it. Eric's breath caught in his throat, it had appeared so suddenly. He and Alison shined their lights on it, while Terry slowed the boat. They slid under it, the sides of the boat scraping on the ragged edges of rock.

Now the channel branched around a rocky impasse. Terry took the course to the right. It curved endlessly, leading them between dark, looming walls that crowded inward as they went, as though threatening to crush them. Terry gasped, but kept the boat moving slowly on as long as their lantern showed that the passage would allow them through.

And then, suddenly, they were in the open again. Their channel emptied out into a placid lake under a spacious, arched ceiling. Alison played her flashlight beam around the edges of the lake. They were smooth and sloping, like a beach of rock.

Terry guided the boat slowly around the edge of the lake. When the lantern picked up a dark object, Eric shouted. "Look! Over there!"

Alison's light traveled over it. "It looks like a coffin!"

"Or a treasure chest?" Terry brought the boat to a stop in front of it.

It was set twenty feet away from them, against the arching wall. They got out, walking carefully on the slippery rocks, and Terry hooked the bowline around a boulder. Then they went cautiously toward the object.

"It sure looks like a coffin," Eric said in a low voice. His skin was prickling. Was this the cave of the monster? Would the monster be lurking somewhere near? Alison held his arm tightly. He held the lantern high, glanced around warily, then went on.

"What would a coffin be doing in here?" Terry reached it first.

Now Eric could see that a piece of light wood lay along the top of the box, words printed on it in red paint. He held his light so they could all read it.

Here lies all that remains of my father,
John T. Roberts, killed this 5th day of
December, 1887, by the monster that
inhabits these waters.

WARNING

The same fate will befall anyone who
tries to recover Scarab's treasure.
THE TREASURE IS CURSED.

Eric felt chills shivering through him.

Alison and Terry looked up at him, their eyes wide with horror, their faces white in the lantern light.

"Shark, probably," Terry said.

Eric swung around, holding the lantern so he could see as much of the lake as possible. Nothing broke the surface of the water. "But the treasure," he said. "It must be down there, in that lake."

"That couldn't be!" Alison said. "Did he mean John Roberts was down there, diving for it?"

"If a shark got him, it has to be in the water someplace." Eric grabbed her hand. "Let's get back to the boat."

Terry's voice was shrill with fear. "If there's a monster shark in there, he could turn over our boat in nothing flat!"

"That happened a long time ago." Eric tried to sound calm. "It couldn't still be here."

"But if one shark was in here, there could be others." Alison's cold fingers gripped his as they headed for the boat.

"John Roberts was too old to be diving for a chest full of heavy stuff," Eric said. "Anyway, he was the one that hid the treasure here. He wouldn't have just dropped it into the lake. It would be too hard to get out. So it's here someplace. His son probably didn't touch it."

"Because he thought it was cursed," Alison said. "I would, too." She clambered into the boat, drawing her jacket closer around her.

"Well, sharks don't come up on land, so it's got to be in the water." Terry tossed the bowline into the boat.

"Maybe there's an island someplace in the lake." Eric tried to see, but the lantern illuminated only a few feet around them. "Let's take the boat out toward the center."

"I don't know," Terry said hesitantly. "What about that shark?"

Once more, Eric could almost see the treasure. A picture

was forming again in the back of his mind, of jewels gleaming against a bed of gold. It was here! Somewhere close! He couldn't just turn away. He had to see it, touch it. "There's no shark here," he said impatiently. "We haven't seen any. Besides, how can we live with ourselves if we're this close to our treasure and don't try to find it?"

"OK," Terry said. "OK. I guess you're right." He started the motor, heading the boat out toward the center of the lake. "I just hope that monster died a long ago."

"So do I!" Alison said, but she managed a smile.

Eric was relieved. He was more afraid than he'd let on, but his yearning for the treasure was strong. He held the lantern as high as he could and scanned the waters eagerly.

The light gleamed on something yellow, not far from their path. "There!" his voice quivered. "Over there!" He nearly fell out of the boat, trying to get a better look.

Terry swerved the boat toward it. Now they could all see it. A chest, standing on a jut of rock, just above the dark water.

"The treasure!" Alison's light fluttered to join his.

Terry shouted. "The treasure! We've found it!"

The boat swerved crazily toward the tiny island. Eric's heart pulsed in his throat. The chest, made of wood bound with yellow strips of metal, seemed to float on the water like a vision. The boat came so close they could reach out and touch it, making waves that lapped greedily toward the lock that fastened it. Now they were all silent, staring at it.

It's really here, Eric thought. Secure on its rocky perch that has held it like a cupped palm for all these long years! The water whispered around them and the night breeze sighed at the ceiling of the cave as he looked at it in awe.

Then another sound came to him, and his body turned to ice.

There was laughter behind them.

Eric twisted around, his numb fingers nearly dropping the lantern that bumped against his free arm. He clutched it and held it high.

A glowing figure stood on the edge of the lake near the entrance, its laughter ringing weird and wild.

Alison screamed.

The ghost placed hands on hips and its green ring flashed. *"The treasure is mine!"*

"Scarab!" Terry breathed.

Eric was frozen with fear. Here in this eerie cave the ghostly figure was even more terrifying than it had been in the cemetery. But something was tugging his mind, trying to free his thoughts. The treasure. It was right here, beside them. Theirs to take. Anger suddenly surged through him, heating him into boldness. "It's *not* yours!" he roared. "You stole it from us, Scarab!"

The ghost threw back its head and laughed again. *"It is mine!"* the hoarse voice sounded across the water. *"Mine!"* The hand with the ring waved and pointed toward the cave entrance. *"Go!"*

Terry sat immobile at the controls of the boat, his eyes wide and staring. Eric's hand brushed the hot glass of the lantern. He flinched and the light waved. The burn on his flesh brought him back to his senses. He wanted a close look at the figure on the shore. He nudged Terry. "Take the boat over there, beside it," he whispered.

Terry turned to look at him with frightened eyes.

"Go on!"

But Terry seemed unable to move.

The ghost watched for a moment, then started toward them, glowing like a green ember as it moved along the edge of the lake.

And then it slipped.

For a moment it teetered on the slippery rock, waving its arms, trying to balance itself, and then it fell into the dark waters, splashing wildly. A scream rose from it, a high-pitched scream of distress—before it disappeared under the surface.

Without thinking, Eric stood up. He stripped off his jacket and plunged into the water, swimming toward the place where the pirate had fallen. The water was icy, but he was no longer numb. He saw the figure bob up again, arms waving, and in a few more strokes he was beside it, grasping it, maneuvering his arm around the neck so he could backstroke toward the shore. The body struggled briefly, then relaxed in his hold. In a moment he was against the rocky edge, pulling himself up onto the slope, towing the figure with him. When he had it safely on the rocks, he knelt beside it.

The broad-brimmed hat was gone. The beard had fallen off in the water. He looked down on a glimmer of white face, the glow of green clothing.

Terry and Alison had drawn near in the boat, and one of them lifted the lantern so that the light fell on the dripping figure beside him. He could see the pirate boots and the jeweled sword and the lacy shirt where the hand with the emerald ring lay motionless.

And he could see the face clearly.

It was Aunt Barbara.

21 • Greed Finds Its Reward

The clock in the hallway struck midnight. Eric and Alison sat in the glass-walled room, waiting.

Terry was talking on the phone. "Can you come right over, Uncle Dan? I know it's late, but this is an emergency. Something happened to Aunt Barbara. No, she's going to be all right, but she nearly drowned. I can't tell you the whole thing over the phone, there's been too much happening. Yes, James is with her now, but we need you and Aunt Nell here. Thanks. We'll be waiting." He replaced the receiver slowly, and turned to Eric and Alison. "They'll be here soon."

Eric nodded. He stared at Aunt Barbara's empty wheelchair in the corner.

"I don't understand," Alison said for the hundredth time. "I just don't understand."

James came into the room. He was dressed in black, just as he had been hours before, when he was with them unnoticed in the dark cave. He looked tired and sad. He sat heavily in the upholstered chair near them. "She's sleeping now. She'll stay peaceful the rest of the night."

Terry sat on the couch next to Alison. "Can you tell us about it now, James?"

He nodded. "Be a relief to get it off my conscience." He looked at them sorrowfully. "We never planned to hurt you. Mom would never do that. She just meant to frighten you away and keep the treasure for herself. She felt that she'd earned it, that it was rightfully hers." He rubbed his hands together. "As soon as she learned about its existence, she started thinking that way. Uncle Dan had inherited Grandpa's business, and your dad, Terry, was doing well, too. But we had nothing, except this house and a pile of bills we had to struggle to pay. Oh, I could earn enough to keep us comfortable, but there were her medical bills and she wanted to do all sorts of things she couldn't afford. And she told me so often that she was the only one who looked after Grandma and Grandpa when they were ill. The whole responsibility fell on her. But there was no money left for her. Only the house. She resented that."

Terry shook his head sadly. "Everyone thought she wanted to look after my grandparents, because she was such a good person."

"She *is* a good person," Alison said. "But her illness . . . she was always in the wheelchair. I didn't know she was able to walk."

"She wasn't." James said. "She couldn't walk for a long time. But there's nothing physically wrong with her legs. Her illness is psychosomatic."

"What does that mean?" Terry looked puzzled.

"It's her mind that's mixed up. She was driving the car when she had the accident and Grandma was killed, two years ago. She was hurt in the accident too, but when she found out that Grandma had died, she felt guilty. She thought she'd caused it. She couldn't accept that it was only an accident. She had to start seeing a psychiatrist. He told us both that her guilt was making her ill, and that her body was healed."

157

"Do you mean she only thought she was paralyzed?" Alison asked him.

"I don't understand it all, but her guilt made her believe she was really paralyzed. But she was able to walk, and she did when she felt she had to. When she decided to take the treasure for herself."

"So when we started looking for it, she made herself walk?" Eric asked.

James nodded. "She didn't know where it was. You had to find it for her. That's why she followed you to the cemetery, to try to scare you away from it when you found it."

"Did you go with her that time?" Eric asked.

"Not the first time. But I discovered the car was gone, and when she got back, I asked her about it. That was when she told me she meant to take the treasure for herself . . . and for me. I didn't know what to do. She's my mother. I love her. I was surprised to find out she could walk now. Of course, she stayed in her wheelchair because she didn't want you or anyone else to know." He ran his hands through his hair in a nervous gesture. "The second time she went to the cemetery, she asked me to take her, just in case her illness came back suddenly."

"Where did she get the pirate's clothes?" Alison asked. "And the scarab ring?"

"There are a lot of costumes in the playroom. That was one of them. She put florescent paint on it so it would glow in the dark, like a ghost. And the ring has been in the family for years. It was just called the pirate's ring. We didn't know it was Scarab's. Mom thought it was costume jewelry."

"Then tonight, when we went down to the cavern, she asked you to go with her?" Eric asked.

"She asked me to get my friend's boat so we could follow you."

"I thought I heard a motor behind us," Eric said. "But

there were so many echoes in those caves, I couldn't be sure."

James nodded. "We kept our lights out. She wore her black cape with a hood over that costume, so you wouldn't see us. We followed your lights, and then we heard you shouting that you'd found the treasure. That's when I took her into the cave."

"You let her out on the shore and then you hid just behind the entrance," Eric said.

"I was scared stiff, but I couldn't talk her out of it. When I heard her fall in the water, I started the boat, to bring it in and rescue her. But you were swimming for her by that time." He fell silent, twisting his hands in his lap.

Eric felt a surge of sympathy for him. He'd wanted so much to take care of his mother that he'd let her talk him into trying to steal the treasure. But hadn't Eric himself felt something close to the same feeling? He knew that the treasure had filled his own thoughts with greed. He'd wanted to keep it all for himself, just as John Roberts and Aunt Barbara had. They had all made up reasons to justify their greed, but that was the true reason. The thought of the treasure had been too much for them! He felt ashamed. Greed was the real monster in that cave. Greed had killed John Roberts and possessed this sick woman's mind. He would never again let it possess his.

Alison was talking. ". . . and if there's really a shark, it could still be there. We'll have to be careful. And we're going to have to get more equipment to get the treasure chest out of there."

"We'll figure out something," Terry said, "when Uncle Dan and Aunt Nell get here." He smiled at James. "I'm sure Aunt Barbara will get better, now that she knows she can walk again."

"And once we get the treasure out," Alison said, "you could consider making those caves a tourist attraction. Might make loads of money that way!"

James smiled, for the first time that night. It was still a rusty smile, Eric thought, but he knew now there was a good heart behind it. "But I don't think we ought to call it our treasure anymore," he said.

Alison looked mystified. "Why do you say that?"

"Because I think John Roberts's son might have been right. There is a monster in that cave, and it's a lot more dangerous than a shark. Look what it did to John Roberts, and to Aunt Barbara. And I even felt the monster getting to me." He shuddered. "So from now on, what do you say we just call it our chest of antiques?"